CW01085737

Artemisa Cannot Stop Killing People

Daniel J Hainey

FIRST EDITION

Published in 2022 by
GREEN CAT BOOKS
19 St Christopher's
Way Pride Park
Derby
DE24 8JY

www.green-cat.shop

Copyright © 2022 Daniel J Hainey
All rights reserved.
ISBN: 978-1-913794-38-5

No part of this publication may be reproduced
in any form or by any means without the prior
written permission of the publisher.

This book is sold subject to the conditions that
shall not, by way of trade or otherwise, be lent,
resold, hired out, or otherwise circulated
without the publisher's prior consent in any
form of binding other than that in which it is
published and without a similar condition
including this condition being imposed on the
subsequent purchaser.

DEDICATION

Family
Friends
Cider
X

CONTENTS

Chapter One:

Artemisa sat at the back of a lecture hall, bored out of her fucking mind and resisting the urge to start a fight. These meetings were tedious, repetitive and unnecessary, wherever she went death followed; you don't need a meeting for that.

Artemisa reached down to her boot and took out a lighter and a penknife. The hinge on a Zippo lighter was strong and clicking the lid open and closed gave her more enjoyment than listening to what a sweat-drenched C.I.A. agent in a suit that was too big for them had to say.

Artemisa smirked as she saw people at the front begin to get agitated at the sound of the Zippo lid; Artemisa persisted, wanting to see who would rise to the mild annoyance and face the consequences and those who hold their tongue. It wasn't like she had anything to lose.

After five minutes, Artemisa knew something would happen soon. She could see people fidgeting, unable to look at the PowerPoint that was on the projector, they were at breaking point. Artemisa stopped for a minute to watch them relax before she continued.

This was the sin that broke the nun's faith, as one of the agents turned around and screamed at Artemisa who was sitting fifteen rows back, "WILL YOU STOP THAT! FOR THE LOVE OF GOD ALMIGHTY!"

Artemisa stood up, a smile on her face, lighter still being flicked in her right hand. She began climbing over the seats as opposed to walking down the stairs. As she got closer, she said, "Fuck your God Almighty and fuck you. You don't tell me what to do, and if you're not happy with that we can take this outside."

Artemisa saw fear in every face, as prominent as an unsightly spot. She couldn't help but begin to laugh, as she got to the row in front. "Don't seem as brave when I am a row behind you all, any reason for that?"

"Artemisa, please," the sweaty man pleaded.

"Apologise for your outburst and this meeting can resume," Artemisa said calmly.

There was a tense silence, Artemisa knew there was no reason for them to apologise, but she was going to make them apologise regardless.

Eventually a faint, "Sorry," came from the crowd.

"Apology accepted. Mark, you can continue with your monotonous crap."

"It's Callum," the sweaty man muttered.

Artemisa took a seat behind them, and she watched their shoulders tense. She had only been on this military base for two months, but rarely left the aircraft hangar that acted as her residence and prison, only allowed to leave it under approved circumstances. But despite the relatively short amount of time, she had managed to create enemies and gain a level of infamy.

When the meeting was over, the 20 C.I.A. agents left the room and Artemisa's heavily-armed escort arrived to escort her back. Artemisa had gotten to know these men quite well, as much as she detested them; on the one hand, they were just following orders, on the other, she wouldn't hesitate to kill them if an escape opportunity presented itself.

"How is little Becky's fever?" she asked as they walked.

She didn't get a response until they were outside, when her escorts could speak more freely.

"She is well, her older sister however, is fuming she had to cancel a date because of this fever, didn't want it being passed around the school."

"Bet you're so upset she's had to rearrange the date?" Artemisa said, sarcasm evident in every word.

"I'd kill him if I could, he is trouble and will get her into trouble. She is young and dumb."

"If only you knew someone really good at killing, like really good at killing. Can kill with a prolonged touch; can kill with a single punch. Like, so good at killing they're a slave to the U.S. government because they're so good at killing. If you knew someone like that, then your problem might be solved," Artemisa said, in a mockingly thoughtful voice.

Half of her guards camera as proof of death laughed at this, the other half felt uncomfortable and remained silent, averting their eyes from her. Artemisa didn't care, she was hilarious and if they were uncomfortable, then it was because they were helping to keep her a slave, nothing more.

This joke killed the conversation and there was silence for the remainder of the walk.

Artemisa walked into the hangar and slumped down on the bed. *'If only I were bulletproof as well as an excellent killer, I'd be free and living my own life',* she thought bitterly. Now the briefing was over, Artemisa had two options, drink or work out.

Artemisa lived out of a backpack, it was all she was permitted. She had an old Gameboy with a copy of Pokémon, a knife, the lighter and a plain baseball cap. Everything else, as she was constantly reminded, was not hers; the clothes on her back were bought for her whenever she moved from one base to another, and they moved her around. A lot.

It was easier for her overlords to buy her new clothes than provide her with the ability to wash and dry her clothes.

Thinking about this started to piss Artemisa off, so she moved to where her weights and the gym equipment were and started working out.

With every rep she thought about escape routes, ways to avoid the perimeter security; cutting out her tracking implant, although painful, would be easy. What she would do after, Artemisa didn't know nor care. She was getting sick of being flown around the world and ordered to kill.

If she was doing it out of her own free will, being paid a high wage and was free to live her life, then things would be different.

The propaganda Artemisa had been fed from birth, about everything she was doing being for the greater good, for the safety and security of all western citizens, not just Americans, had worn off; she was smarter, older, stronger and she was more determined than ever to live her life, one way or another she would be free.

When sweat dropped onto the weights and Artemisa had no energy to be pissed off at the world, at the U.S. military and at her life, the curse she was born with, so, burnt out and fucked off she did as she always did, she showered and cracked a can of beer and slumped down on the worn-out old sofa; there was nothing else for her to do anyway.

The next morning, Artemisa awoke to her name being screamed. She lifted her bleary head from a pillow and looked around, her escorts were there but they weren't alone.

They stood with someone who had to be a general, even with one eye open she saw his stance; he looked like the personification of arrogance.

"What now?" she groaned.

"Get up, we need you," he ordered.

"All of you lot fuck off and let me get showered and

changed then," Artemisa said, not lifting her head from the pillow.

"Now."

"Come get me out of bed then," Artemisa challenged.

There was a short pause and he said, "You have twenty minutes to get ready."

Artemisa showered, changed, collected her things and met her escorts outside.

"What is going on?"

They were silent and walked Artemisa to the lecture hall and left her at the door without a word.

"Thanks for the conversation, dickbags," Artemisa muttered as she entered, just loud enough for them all to hear her.

She made her way to the back of the hall as she usually did and slumped into a seat. One-by-one, she watched F.B.I. agents and soldiers file in and take their seats and wait.

"It's almost like you didn't need to get me out of bed until we were ready to fucking go!" Artemisa shouted over the muttering and talking. She did this to keep her reputation but was curious as to why the F.B.I. were here.

The general, who had woken her up did not look amused, but Artemisa was pleased to see she was getting under his skin. It took a further ten minutes until Callum turned up.

"About time," Artemisa moaned, taking her lighter out of her boot with full intentions of continuing her aggravation from the day before.

"The mission has been moved up 48 hours. We have new intelligence, meaning the time to act is now."

Artemisa rolled her eyes. They could skip all of this, put a photo on the screen of who needed to die, and they could escort her to an aeroplane and be done with it.

Instead, Artemisa sat playing with her lighter until they got to the mission report that she actually needed to pay attention to. They flashed photos of eight Nazis. Artemisa understood why the F.B.I. were here, this was a mission on American soil. They just needed her to do the killing.

Artemisa studied their faces intently. Not that she got paid, but she would have bet that after she moved in, there would be a gas explosion, or a homemade bomb would go off to hide the evidence.

"Artemisa, are you clear on what you have to do?" Callum asked.

Everyone shifted round to look at her, as she said, "Maximum casualties but make sure those eight are dead. Same shit, different location. Enter. Kill. Leave."

"Show your superior some respect," the general said before Callum could speak.

Artemisa, losing her temper, took her knife out of the boot and threw it just over the general's shoulder. Before the knife could clatter to the floor, there were guns pointing at her from every direction.

Artemisa put her feet back up, completely unconcerned with the guns now pointing in her direction. "Do you want me to kill them or not?"

"Wheels up in 30," Callum said sheepishly.

Artemisa trudged down the stairs, still ignoring the guns trained on her, collected her knife and left the room. She walked, bag over her shoulder towards the buildings near the base's runway.

She slipped on a bulletproof vest and began plaiting her blonde hair from the rushed bun she put it in this morning, put on a helmet and waited for the others to arrive.

Artemisa half-wished one of these missions would go wrong, but the U.S. wouldn't allow her to die, she knew that even if she got sloppy and ended up getting shot, they would pour every resource, every dollar into ensuring she lived.

Nobody looked at her or said as much as a word to her as the plane took off, heading to whichever state they needed to go to. When Artemisa was younger she used to enjoy plane journeys. The force of take-off and landing was exciting, but now they were just a commute to a job she fucking hated.

Local law enforcement had cars waiting for them as the plane landed on a dirt airstrip.

As they departed the plane, they were given earpieces.

"Listen up, fuckheads. Listen to me and you all get to go home to your lives and family, don't listen to me and there will be children in little suits crying beside your coffins."

"Why is the freak in charge?" one of the agents asked.

Artemisa sat down and they all stopped to look at her. "Well, if Mr Shrivel Cock thinks they can do a better job then I will stay here."

"I apologise for that outburst, but we need to move," a different man said, attempting in vain to keep the peace.

"He'll apologise with his life, anyone else have an issue with me leading this mission?"

Silence followed this question, and after a few minutes Artemisa said, "That is what I thought. Now follow me and let's go."

She led the way and delegated who would ride with her, as seemingly nobody wanted to get in her car, and they were off. Artemisa was not driving, as she was not paying attention to where they needed to go.

"We are a mile and a half away," the agent Artemisa assigned to drive said. "Am I correct to assume you want us to pull over?"

"Yes," Artemisa said. "You've been on missions with me before."

"Yes, sir."

"Good."

They stopped the cars and Artemisa led them through the fields towards the farm.

"Why do we have to approach from so far away?" someone asked.

"Because I said so, as I always say: if you have a problem with how I run an operation then say it to my face and I'll listen to your points."

Silence again, and Artemisa led them onwards. When they approached the farm, Artemisa signalled them to surround the building and wait on her signal.

Skulking towards the target, she asked, "Do we have a visual on how many are inside?"

"Registering fifteen in the barn and twelve in the house," came a voice.

"I'll take the barn with five of you, the rest take the house, confirm the relevant eight are dead before you head back. If one of them gets away, then you deal with me. Everyone understand?"

When Artemisa had the replies she was expecting, they moved in.

Artemisa signalled for two of them to come over and give her the necessary boost to an upper window, she climbed in and surveyed the situation.

"Move on three," Artemisa whispered as she spotted six of the eight targets.

Artemisa leapt down from her elevated position as the men stormed the door, blocking all exits. The Nazis had their backs turned, so they didn't notice Artemisa launching herself until it was too late.

With several of them now on the ground, Artemisa scrambled to her knees and began throwing punches to the ones she had knocked down. As soon as her fist connected with their faces and their heads bounced off the hay-and-wood-strewn floor, they were dead.

Within seconds she was back on her feet, and she began throwing punches; with every punch that connected the recipient fell to the ground, dead.

Artemisa threw ten punches and there were ten dead bodies on the ground around her. The five she brought with her took down the other five, who had decided to run as opposed to fight. When the dust settled, Artemisa looked up and they all stood looking at her aghast.

"You've all worked with me before, this shouldn't be shocking to you," Artemisa snorted, rolling her eyes at them. "Go check on those in the house, make sure they've not fucked up."

Artemisa took photos of four of them, before leaving the bodies behind her and moving towards the house, without a second glance at bodies strewn across the barn floor. It was a short walk from the barn to the house and although she saw bodies of Nazis, there were no bodies of the agents who were accompanying her on this mission; always a promising sign and it meant she had it easier when she returned to her military captors.

She entered the house to find that there were only four left alive, the four that needed confirmation of their deaths.

"Why are they still alive?" she asked the room at large, ordering some of the surplus federal agents back towards the cars.

"We are attempting to extract information," a sneering voice said.

"Was that the mission?" Artemisa asked the room at large. "Or was the mission to kill them?"

Artemisa struck three of them and they were dead. Dead where they knelt. The last one alive began to weep. Artemisa stared at him, emotionless. She was tired and he was just another photo. She needed to take a photo of him with her camera as proof of death. He didn't need to cry, as soon as she touched his skin, he would die, he just needed to get on with it.

Artemisa punched him, took the necessary photos and ordered everyone back towards the cars.

"That was stupid, we could have gotten useful information from him," the agent who had been making sneering comments all day said.

Artemisa knew what the punishment was for what she was considering, and for the briefest moment she held an internal debate as to whether or not it was worth it. Once the debate was concluded, she took a few short steps towards the agent, and taking the gun from his holster she turned off the safety and shot him in the foot.

The agent fell and rolled around the floor clutching his boot, screaming as if the rapture was here. Artemisa announced, "The cars leave in 10 minutes, don't be late."

She continued walking, remaining calm and not letting her temper get the best of her during the whole experience, just wanting to be back in her hangar, with a drink and some peace and quiet.

Two federal agents aided the one she shot back to the cars and once they were all accounted for, they began the drive back to the airstrip.

They were back to ignoring Artemisa now the mission was over; Artemisa didn't care. She had completed her mission, her Gameboy had plenty of battery life left in it and she could now look forward to some solitude and a quiet drink before the nightmare continued tomorrow.

They landed, two of the federal agents escorted the one Artemisa had shot towards a medic and Artemisa allowed herself to be escorted back to her confinement, which unfortunately was the only place she could call home.

She showered and sank down on the old worn out sofa next to her gym equipment, glass in her hand and Gameboy in the other, resisting the urge to scream.

Artemisa had barely drank half of her glass contents when she was interrupted by the general, and Callum, looking as sweaty as he always did.

"The mission is over, leave me alone," Artemisa requested, not looking at them.

"We need to check a few things from the mission debrief with you."

"We can do that tomorrow," Artemisa dismissed them, not looking up.

"One of the agents sustained a bullet wound to the foot."

"I am aware."

"How did it happen?"

"Don't know, I took a smaller group towards the barn, cleared there and made my way to the house."

"Artemisa, did you shoot the agent in the foot?"

Artemisa ignored them for as long as possible before she said, "I am not even going to dignify that with an answer. You told me to go there and kill everyone and get verification that eight of them were dead. They are dead. That is all that matters."

"Thank you, Artemisa," Callum replied, turning to leave.

"Just one minute," the general blurted, stopping Callum from leaving. "That doesn't answer the question asked."

"It does, unless you want a knife thrown at you, then accept the answer, this time she won't miss," Callum advised, before Artemisa could issue a similar threat.

Artemisa realised later that evening that her supply of alcohol was running low, so she hatched a daring plan to break her curfew, go across to the shop and get some more.

Artemisa checked to see whether or not she was being guarded, which was less than ideal but had been known to happen. With no guards on either side of the doorway, she began to walk. Keeping to the shadows, she walked through the base, barely making a sound.

She doubted anyone would be watching her tracker, so she would be back without anyone realising she had ever left. She avoided a couple who were on an evening walk and a group of kids playing baseball in the street, and made it to the shop without being spotted.

She had 'borrowed' Callum's credit card a few days after she arrived on the base, and she was about to put it to good use, as she slipped out and made her way across the base, dodging those on patrol.

Artemisa finally entered the base shop. She picked up some beer, cider and a bottle of bourbon whiskey along with some sweets, chocolate and biscuits and walked to the counter and tapped the bell on the counter.

The store assistant had clearly been warned about Artemisa when she arrived, as she could see fear in his eyes when they met hers. Artemisa wasn't going to kill him for not selling her the alcohol, after all she was 19, but it would be easier than making a scene.

He shakily scanned each item and accepted the credit card from Artemisa and bid her farewell with a shaky voice. Artemisa felt particularly smug as she left the shop and made her way back. She avoided everyone and slipped back into the hangar, pleased with her stealth.

She put the cans and bottles next to her bed and paused, one of her weights was not where she left it. Artemisa pretended to be removing the cardboard from the cans as she took the knife out of her boot.

She straightened up, cider can in one hand and her knife in the other.

"I'm going to be really annoyed if you kill me," a familiar voice called out.

Artemisa turned and looked to the shadows, a rare smile on her face. "You've come a long way to move my weights around, Hannah."

One of the few people who treated Artemisa like somewhat of a human stepped towards her and sat down on the side of Artemisa's bed. "Who has been buying you booze?"

"Callum," Artemisa explained, offering them the bottle as she cracked the can ring pull.

"Surprised at that," Hannah said, accepting the bottle.

"Well, he lent me his credit card."

"Oh, for God's sake, I am going get it in the ear when he finds out."

"He deserves it."

Hannah didn't disagree with this, and just sipped their drink to avoid answering.

"I've been working on a mission involving you," Hannah announced after a short while, "the only issue is it means you trust someone else."

Artemisa looked at Hannah with skepticism written all over her face. "What is he going to give me to prove he is human?"

"I've already told him to bring something."

"What is the mission?"

"Let's take a walk," Hannah suggested.

Artemisa and Hannah left the hangar and began to walk around the base.

"What is the mission?" Artemisa asked.

"I don't know yet, all you need to know is it will be called

Operation Phoenix," Hannah said, in a voice so low Artemisa struggled to hear them. "We're going to fake your death, and get you out of this military slavery."

Artemisa stopped, looking at Hannah. "Why?"

"For the same reason I gave you a Gameboy with a game you could pour hours into, for the reason I am trying to reduce the restrictions on you when you are here. You're a human being, and you deserve to be treated as such, and now I am in the position within the C.I.A. to put a plan into action."

Artemisa didn't really know how to respond to this, but was also suspicious.

After a long while, she eventually said, "Who do you need to bring in to help with this?"

"A colleague of mine, called Richard Cherry."

"Do you trust him?"

"I do."

"Why do you need his help?"

"It is a massive undertaking, we would need to get you false passports, I.D. cards, bank accounts, safety deposit boxes in banks. Plus, we then need to hide your escape and get you back to the country without being noticed. Not to mention, he'll help us find a mission in which you'd be able to escape, and it would be plausible."

"When?"

"You're in?"

"Obviously."

"Good, we need you to play your part."

"What is my part?"

"Not to shoot any more federal agents on missions. Not to kill any, but be aggressive, we need them to dislike you but not actively hate you."

"Given what is at stake, I can do that."

"And not a word to anyone."

"Yeah, because so many people talk to me around here."

"Well, when they do, try not to offer to kill their daughter's boyfriend."

Artemisa rolled her eyes so hard she almost tripped up a kerb. As she staggered, she said, "Fine, I'll sulk in silence until the time comes, and complete missions like a good slave."

"There we go. Thanks for the drink, Artemisa," Hannah smiled, before they escorted Artemisa back toward her hangar in silence.

That night, Artemisa drank alone, not in anger but in a fiery determination that for the first time in her life, there was hope for something better, hope that she would be more than the U.S. government's killing machine.

When Artemisa wasn't needed, she was confined to the

hangar, so the next couple of days were a blur of repetitive boredom; work out, combat practice, play her console, drink, sleep and then repeat.

Five days after her covert meeting with Hannah, her workout was interrupted by her escort, who informed her she was required. Ignoring the urge to throw her plate at them, she picked up her steak and followed them, ripping at the meat with her teeth obnoxiously as they walked.

"Do you have to eat it like that?" one of them asked her, as a speck of steak sauce flew off the steak and onto their shoulder.

"Do you have to interrupt my workout, meaning I won't get to eat?" Artemisa retorted.

Silence concluded their walk and Artemisa was once again directed to the back of the lecture hall. She took her seat, took out her lighter and waited for everyone to file into the room.

Artemisa watched, her curiosity slightly above zero as Special Forces and C.I.A. agents walked in; she normally worked with either/or as opposed to both.

"This is an off-the-books, covert mission," the stranger at the front of the room said.

'No shit', Artemisa thought, given the fact she was in the room.

"This is also a stealth mission, minimal casualties, minimal noise."

'How dull', Artemisa thought.

"This is of paramount importance to the safety of the entire western world."

'Oh great, another assassination mission', Artemisa mused, a gloomy expression on her face. These missions bored her, since she grew wise to the propaganda she had been fed, since she was old enough to pay attention to a TV screen or read a book.

Artemisa watched them justify why the discovery of oil meant that the country's president now needed to be murdered and replaced by a pro-American counterpart.

All Artemisa needed was the blueprint of the presidential estate, how they were going to get her in and how they were going to get her out.

It took 45 minutes till they got to the information Artemisa needed. The man delivering the presentation stopped about a sentence in, as one of the special forces had their arm in the air.

"Yes?" he asked impatiently.

"We haven't been told who and how we are to take out the target, sir," he said.

"I am aware of that, your job, soldier, is to get our agent in and get them out," he said, indicating Artemisa at the back of the room.

Artemisa waved in mock enthusiasm. She noticed the

special forces scowl, as the prim and proper men looked at the 19-year-old slouched in her chair, her leg over the armrest next to her.

"Why is she being trusted with such a high-value target?"

"Walk up here and find out," Artemisa snapped, lighting her lighter and waving the flame about.

"Artemisa, don't do that. If he is to die, it'll be in combat, not being shown up by you," the man delivering the brief warned.

Artemisa let out a rare smile as she watched the others face the front with disgruntled looks.

"There is a tight extraction window, you'll all need to play your parts and stick to your roles, perfectly. No playing the hero, keep the path clear for Artemisa, that is your only objective. Are we all clear?"

Murmurs rippled through the lecture halls in response. They didn't seem too pleased about their roles in the mission being relegated.

"We are waiting for contact from our people on the ground, wheels up anytime in the next 72 hours. Stay prepared, stay close and stay sober." His eyes flicked to Artemia with the last instruction, and she stuck her middle finger up as a response.

Artemisa waited for them all to leave before she stood up and went to leave. As she walked down the stairs, she noticed that her escort had also left.

Artemisa smiled and left the lecture hall. Not wanting to give anyone an excuse to shoot her, she headed towards the door.

"I'll escort you back," the man who delivered the brief said cheerily, jogging to catch up to Artemisa.

"I don't really have a choice," Artemisa said. "I didn't catch your name?"

"I didn't give my name," he replied, in a happy, joyful voice that grated on Artemisa.

"Aren't you a riddle, ooh, I have no name but am a knobhead, what am I?" Artemisa retorted.

"Name's Richard Cherry,"

Artemisa turned and scowled at him, she didn't attempt to hide the suspicion on her face. She stared at him for a while before saying slowly, "You should have a present for me."

"It is already in your hangar," he chuckled.

Artemisa walked in silence with the man, waiting to see if he would strike a conversation or just let her enjoy the silence. He let her enjoy the silence and she was grateful for it; Artemisa always believed you could tell a lot about a man by how often he interrupted a silence so everyone could hear his voice.

He bid Artemisa farewell at the hangar door and left her to her own devices. Artemisa made her way over to her bed and slumped down.

As she did, she felt something under her pillow. It was a small box. Artemisa opened it, curious as to what Richard Cherry had given her to earn her trust.

As she looked in the box, it was a pair of noise-cancelling earphones and an MP3 player. Artemisa had a look through the hundreds of bands and all of the genres.

Artemisa spent the evening with her Gameboy in hand and music playing. It was an enjoyable way to spend her evening, as much as she still distrusted Richard Cherry; he had a long way to go till he was on Hannah's level.

Artemisa was asleep for no more than three hours when she was awoken and told she was needed. She changed and packed at a reasonable speed and followed her escort.

"It's show time," Richard explained to her, as special forces scrambled all around her.

"Okay," Artemisa shrugged, nonplussed.

She sat contentedly as the others prepped everything. She didn't need instruments of death, she *was* an instrument of death, so watching the others clean guns and check ammunition bemused her.

When special forces had finally stopped wasting valuable time, they boarded the plane and prepped for take-off.

Once she was in the air, in order to preserve the battery

life in her MP3 and Gameboy, she decided to annoy the people sitting closest to her.

"Are any of you missing any special events for this?" she asked the plane at large. "Anyone missing a kid's birthday? Wedding anniversary? Seeing their daughter off to prom?"

They looked at her but none of them said anything.

"There is no way all of you are single, kid-less, bachelors! By a very minimum, at least one of you could be classed as not that ugly," Artemisa said loudly and obnoxiously.

The people looking at her began to glare at her and still none of them said anything.

'*None of them are biting*,' Artemisa thought.

After a short pause, she pointed at one of them who was sitting near her and said, "You look like you're missing out on threatening the boy who is going to finger a child of yours tonight? Why the long face?"

"Shut the hell up," he snapped eventually.

"Sorry, I'll get us back quickly so you can get home and find them in bed together," Artemisa said, as if she was doing them a genuine favour.

The man stood up and looked at Artemisa, who smiled and stood up. He towered over her and Artemisa smiled wide.

"Touched a nerve have I, big boy?" Artemisa taunted,

stepping forward.

"Shut the hell up, freak."

Artemisa watched his finger twitch towards the gun on his hip. "Try it, big boy!" She shouted so more people could hear, "You've got to ask yourself, how quick do you think you are; can you draw and fire in the time it takes me to throw a punch at you? You got the balls to try it? I BEG you to try it."

Artemisa's fist was clenched, but the two on either side of him grabbed him and sat him back down in his seat. Artemisa, seeing this, also took her seat, smiling wide.

She looked at the two who had pulled him back and said, "You two are smart! I respect that."

"It isn't prom season," one of them explained to Artemisa.

"When is prom season? I wouldn't really know, just usually on missions someone is always moaning about missing some family thing that is special."

Nobody replied to her and Artemisa fell into silence, reminding herself that she needed them to be annoyed at her, as opposed to ready to kill her; it was, after all, a fine balance.

She got bored shortly after and was wondering what she could do to pass the time, when the opportunity presented itself as one of them took a pack of cards out of their bag.

"Are you dealing me in?" she asked, as one of them began dealing cards.

They looked at her but none of them dealt her cards or spoke to her, instead they were pretending that she did not exist.

"Well fuck you lot!" She huffed, "Just be careful I don't mistake you for this president dude."

Artemisa expected a reaction, but not the reaction she got; the man who had challenged her earlier stood up and with a trembling hand, withdrew his side arm from its holster and screamed, with a crack in his voice, "SHUT. THE. FUCK. UP!"

"Or what?" Artemisa asked curiously. "What about me frightens you, big boy?"

"Artemisa, sit the fuck down and play on your Gameboy. Taylor, sit back down and shut up before you spend the rest of your career scrubbing statues with your toothbrush," Richard Cherry shouted over all of them.

Artemisa took her seat and pulled out her Gameboy, and Taylor was disarmed and forced back into his seat.

Artemisa sat, Gameboy in hand with her headphones in. Never motionless, her legs bounced as she waited for the plane to land; the sooner the plane landed and the mission started, the sooner she was back in her hangar away from everyone else.

"Touchdown in five minutes. Prep your gear," was the call

from Richard Cherry.

Artemisa saved her game, took off her headphones and began cracking her knuckles. Artemisa didn't need guns and scopes, all she needed was time, silence and nobody to get in her fucking way.

"Artemisa, you follow their orders till they get you in the compound. Once inside, they will only be there to let you know if there is anyone coming."

"I know the mission, Richard," Artemisa growled, exasperatedly.

"Follow their orders," he repeated.

Artemisa nodded and followed them off the plane.

All Artemisa had to do was kill one person. It was a simple job, she didn't understand why there was all this fuss.

"Artemisa, can you hear us?" a voice asked, coming through her earpiece.

"Stealth mission," she whispered, "but yes, tell the sniper team to eliminate, and the ground team to hide the body, and we can get this done quickly."

She could feel them hating her, but she did not give a shit. None of them could do what she could do, so they either aided her or they perished. You didn't get in the way of death, and she was death.

They aided her over the barbed-wire fence, and she made her way through the grounds and into the sprawling mansion. Knowing they would do their jobs, she just needed to hide when told and go when told to go.

"Artemisa, head through the door to your left, there are five heat signatures ahead," a voice muttered in her ear.

She complied with the suggestion, knowing the mission depended on their cohesiveness. She headed through the door and up the spiralling staircase, until she came out two floors above.

"Head down the corridor until the last door on the left," the same voice said.

Artemisa knew this was the bedroom she needed to enter but didn't like the idea of just walking through the bedroom door.

"How much time do I have to pick the lock?" she whispered.

"Two minutes to pick, then the guards will see you."

"And you fuckers were worried this would be a difficult mission," Artemisa scoffed.

She took out her tools, picked the lock and slipped into the bedroom. She was light on her feet as she crept across the bedroom towards the bed where the couple were sleeping.

For the first time on these missions, she felt pity for the wife of the man she was there to kill; waking up next to the man she had loved for so many years, because

America wanted oil. However, there was no point in worrying about it, if she didn't kill them then someone else would; the more missions she completed, the sooner she was to escape from her personal hellscape, with the mission Hannah was preparing.

She crept across to the sleeping man and put her hand on his forehead. For a solid minute she left it there, feeling the life drain from him until he was dead.

"Your way out is clear," the voice said.

Artemisa left the room, relocked the door, and began to make her way out of the mansion; the easy part was done, now she needed to ensure she was not detected. Forty-five minutes later, she made her way out of the compound. She regrouped with the troops, and they made their way back to the aircraft.

When they were all aboard and the plane took off, there was a collective sigh of relief.

When they were safely airborne and out of enemy airspace, Artemisa reached into her bag and pulled out the bottle of whiskey she had bought with Callum's credit card.

Artemisa held the bottle to the heavens and said, "To a successful mission, to friendships forged in secret, to Taylor getting home in time to threaten the lad who is fingering his daughter." She took a swig before offering the bottle to the special forces soldier sitting opposite her.

"I'll drink to the successful mission," he said, accepting the bottle and taking a sip.

He passed the bottle on; it was accepted by some and rejected by others, until it eventually made its way to Taylor.

"Fuck off," he said, glumly.

"Drink," Artemisa insisted, "It might give you a personality."

He didn't accept the bottle, instead he glared at Artemisa.

"Drink and I won't mention your daughter again," Artemis said.

At this, Taylor took the bottle and took a sip, grimaced and coughed before handing it begrudgingly back to Artemisa, hoping this would shut her up.

"See, if I knew we just had to assassinate the leader of a foreign nation together for us to become friends, then I would have made us stop in every other country," Artemisa laughed, "Richard, make us land in the nearest country, let's kill their leader now we are all friends."

Calling each other friends was pushing it, they made it very clear for the duration of the flight. Artemisa didn't care, she could drink, she had her Gameboy, she had pissed off everyone around her; all in all, it was a successful mission.

"What are you playing?" the lad who first accepted the

whiskey off her asked her a few hours later.

"Pokemon," Artemisa said.

"Do you only have one game?"

"Yeah. I don't get a wage. I have to rely on donations and for some reason, nobody has reasoned that I would be less annoying, and happier and calmer if I had an outlet."

This was followed by silence. This didn't surprise Artemisa, but she hoped it would lead to more Gameboy Pokemon games.

They eventually landed stateside and Artemisa was met by an escort to lead her back to the hangar.

She plugged her Gameboy and music player onto charge and collapsed onto her bed, barely taking off any of her clothes before she fell asleep.

When Artemisa awoke and showered, she was met by her escort who, once again in silence, escorted her to the lecture hall in which she spent far too much of her time.

She sat at the back, the Special Forces and C.I.A. agents sat at the front as they watched a news report on the events happening around the world.

"Wow, it's almost like nobody was expecting a healthy fifty-something year old to die in their sleep," Artemisa remarked.

Artemisa noticed at least three people snigger at her comments and she couldn't help but laugh. If they were going to destabilise countries, the least they could do was laugh about it.

"You have done the western world a service in the past 48 hours."

"See!" Artemisa exclaimed. "The entire western world we have done a service to and still some of you wouldn't share a celebratory drink with me."

A few chuckles spread here and there but the vast majority of the room remained silent.

Once the debrief was finished, they all began to leave the hall. As Artemisa was leaving the hall, she bumped into the same special forces soldier from the night before. As he apologised she felt something slip into her pocket.

Artemisa walked with her escort back to her hangar, with her heart beating even faster. She slammed the door in her face and practically ran to her bed, eagerness and anticipation flowing through her blood. She swapped her old game and let out a rare gasp of excitement as she put in the new game.

Artemisa made a mental note that there were now three people she would not kill, Hannah, Richard Cherry, and Unnamed Soldier with a nice face.

Chapter Two:

Artemisa must have stayed awake for at least 30 hours with her new game, exhilarated by the thought that she was considered as more than a killing slave by more than two people.

When she eventually allowed herself to sleep, she wished that the next mission would be the mission where she escaped from her prison.

Much to Artemisa's annoyance, her next mission was four weeks later. What made her more irate, her next mission was not called Operation Phoenix, instead it was a mission about killing pirates who were planning on taking over a tourist cruise ship.

"Who is leading this mission?" Artemisa asked from the back of the room. "I see new faces, I see inexperienced faces, I wanna know who I can work with!"

"Campbell will lead this mission!" Richard Cherry answered. "Don't have a problem with it and follow orders."

"Campbell can suck my balls, I want a team I know, where are the people from the last mission?" Artemisa responded.

Guns were fixed on Artemisa, she didn't give a fucking shit. She was making her point.

"Answer me, you dumb fuck! I don't trust anyone who hasn't worked with me before. Where are those from the last mission? Get them!"

"Artemisa, you will work with new people as we require it, they are on a different mission. SIT DOWN."

"Listen, Cherry, my missions work on a tight schedule, I cannot handle rookies."

"You need to remember your place. You do as you are told."

At this comment, Artemisa vowed she would kill Richard Cherry after she had gotten her use out of him.

Richard Cherry ignored her and in seven hours, Artemisa was aboard a plane with this Campbell and his troops.

"So, fellas, are you gonna talk to me or are you gonna be little bitches like Taylor's troops? Do you know them? They were dicks but proficient, I need you lot to be the same but without being dicks!" Artemisa asked the plane at large, whilst in the air.

Silence followed... given Artemisa hadn't received instructions to fuck Campbell's troops off, she decided to make them hate her.

Artemisa offered snacks around, offered to swap stories of her slavery but none of them seemed to care and none of them engaged with her. Artemisa tried her tested and true routine of asking if any of them were missing family events in order to get them on her side.

Eventually Artemisa shouted, "Listen, either I am about to kill all of you, or you are about to talk to me and show me some trust."

After 20 minutes or so, Artemisa sat, relaxed, listening and thanking those who told her stories, making mental notes on which husbands to kill.

She made a note with pen and scrap of paper that she needed to think of new ways to antagonise people. Artemisa gave up and turned her attention back to the Gameboy until the pilot indicated they were ready.

"Listen up, you overpaid fucks," Artemisa said, looking at the new faces. "Follow all commands and we all survive, if you think of disobeying me then you lot are about to die."

"Two minutes," Richard Cherry called.

"We go in fast; we go in hostile. Those pirates do not make it within a sniper's distance of that cruise ship. Am I clear?"

"Clear," Campbell muttered.

"Good. Check your parachutes, let's go."

Artemisa remembered the exhilaration she felt the first time she jumped out of a plane. Even now, hating every single minute of her life, she still loved the dive out of the plane, gravity pulling her towards the ground. The last possible moment, she pulled the cord.

The night sky was the camouflage that they needed to not be detected, and Artemisa removed her parachute just before she landed in the water.

She climbed up onto the ladder and up onto the back deck of the boat.

Artemisa engaged the pirates before her special force companions had joined her on the deck.

Despite the mutual dislike, nobody could complain they were not effective. Artemisa didn't need guns, only her fists, but together they got the job done and the extraction team pulled up alongside the boat 30 minutes later to escort them back to the plane.

Artemisa was tired, she knew the flight back to the U.S. was going to be long and she craved sleep. She could not sleep on an aeroplane and was not about to fall asleep surrounded by U.S. special forces who could kill her in an instant and get away with it with no consequences.

So Artemisa forced herself to stay awake; the others slept, watched movies on their phones, whatever normal people did.

When Artemisa eventually collapsed onto her bed she fell asleep, fully clothed and on top of the covers, and hoped that nobody would wake her for a few days.

In fact, nobody spoke to Artemisa for over three weeks, which suited her perfectly. She managed to catch up on sleep, work out and enjoy her own company for a while.

Artemia knew that she could do things nobody else could do, but it didn't mean they could put her on any mission, if it wasn't one where her talents could be used then what was the point.

Artemisa didn't understand how much work was needed to help her fake her death but knew she wanted Operation Phoenix to give her a chance at a new life.

Four missions and three months later, Artemisa was working out when she was interrupted by Hannah.

"We've got a mission. Let's go?"

"*A* mission or *The* mission," Artemisa asked, weight still in hand.

"You'll be briefed on the mission," Hannah said, formally, which made Artemisa think that Hannah was not alone.

Artemisa didn't want to take the risk, so she packed her Gameboy, games, headphones and MP3, her entire life into her backpack, and left the hangar.

Artemisa walked with Hannah, a general she didn't recognise, and Richard Cherry.

"This feels different, what is this mission?" Artemisa asked.

"All in due time," Hannah said.

Artemisa took a seat at the back of the lecture hall and watched as both Commander Taylor and Commander Campbell walked in with their men and took their seats.

"What you are about to see cannot leave this room, this is as covert as they come. If you feel like you cannot complete this mission, you will be allowed to walk away from the commanders," Hannah said, once they were all seated.

This got everyone's attention, even Artemisa sat up a little straighter.

"This is Operation Phoenix," Hannah said, as she changed the slide of the PowerPoint to a photo of a man.

A gasp went around the room. This puzzled Artemisa, as she had never seen the man before in her life; clearly, she was in the minority.

"This is Elliot Dusk, for those who do not know, Silicon Valley billionaire, his dad owns an emerald mine in South Africa. The mission is to eliminate Elliot Dusk; his assets are to be reclaimed by the U.S. government. His personal computers, tablets and phones are to be destroyed. His death is the number one priority, Elliot Dusk needs to die before his juvenile behaviour manipulates the stock market further. The commanders and Artemisa will be briefed separately on the rest of the mission." Richard Cherry continued, "Once eliminated, all emeralds, all assets will be collected, boxed up and put onto transport before his home is destroyed."

"Elliot Dusk is a U.S. citizen, is there a reason for this?" Commander Campbell asked, "The media attention on this will be massive. What are our guarantees that this cannot be traced back to us?"

"The reason is, the general and the C.I.A. suits are telling you. Not like we haven't killed U.S. citizens before," Artemisa, yelled. "What are the mission details? Let's get in, get out."

"The mission details are simple," Hannah said, indicating places on the map. "The men will secure the perimeter. Artemisa, you will clear the building, kill Dusk and signal the commanders once dead. The three of you secure what needs to be secured. Armoured cars and a chopper will arrive. Load up and once they are away you make your way back out."

"Understood," Artemisa said, standing up.

"General, sir, madam. What are we being left in the dark about?"

"Nothing, Commander, you two and Artemisa will be briefed in private," the general said, stepping in, to reiterate the point Richard Cherry had just made.

"Understood, sir."

Artemisa and the two commanders followed the general and Hannah, as Richard continued the mission brief.

The general took the commanders into a room to the right and Artemisa followed Hannah into the room to the left.

Hannah leaned forward so they could speak in a hush. "Once Dusk is killed, go into his office. Once you are in his office, begin seizing the high expensive items, and destroying ALL technology. Cut out your tracker. The official story will then be the commanders, when seeing all of the emeralds, get greedy and kill you in an attempt to steal some of the high-end items for themselves. However, as soon as you see my men walk into the room with you and the commanders, make your way out of the room, claiming you need to check another location."

"Understood. then what?" Artemisa whispered.

"Make your way down this corridor and down the laundry shoot. You'll meet a maid called Alexa, she'll get you to safety."

"Understood. Kill Dusk, destroy all technology, cut out tracker, laundry shoot, Alexa," Artemisa repeated.

"Correct."

"What about the commanders? You said we'll make it look like they tried to kill me and that you have men on this mission as well?"

"Not everyone accompanying you on this mission will be soldiers, some will be spies. They've got their mission. Their mission is to kill the commanders and ensure we get what we need out of the mansion. Once you are with Alexa."

"Understood," Artemisa nodded. "What do we need from the mansion?"

"You don't need to worry about that."

This intrigued Artemisa, but she didn't say anything. They were keeping secrets from her, meaning that this Elliot Dusk must be doing some awful things, but she couldn't focus on that. She was so close to freedom.

She and Hannah left the room. "You're not to leave your hangar until it's time, are we clear?" Hannah said, a lot more formal.

Artemisa nodded.

When Artemisa was in her hangar, she sat down on her bed for what would be the last time. As she sat, she noticed something under her pillow.

Pulling it out, she saw a file with her name on it. Artemisa opened it, her eyes widened as it had the names of everyone who was involved in her capture, everyone who knew what she could do, photos and names, the complete history of her being in the position she had been in since her birth. This file was her life.

Artemisa studied the file in depth. Reading everything, both redacted and non-redacted, she scribbled down the key bits of information and stuffed the file in a secure location on her person.

It was harrowing reading, yet it gave Artemisa food for thought and gave her something to do that wasn't just pacing up and down.

Eventually she was escorted onto the plane, and they took off for South Africa. She was quiet, her leg bounced as it normally did, she did not show emotion. She sat watching the men play poker with imaginary chips, absorbing how to play the game.

Even the commanders were quiet. They didn't join in with the poker or speak to each other. In fact they didn't do anything other than shooting her dirty looks occasionally. It seems they weren't happy with having new soldiers under their command.

Artemisa had to remind herself that not all of them were soldiers, and she was not meant to know the difference between the ones that were and the ones who were there as C.I.A. spies.

Artemisa felt nauseous, a feeling she had not felt before a mission in a long time. They had moulded her to not feel such trivial things as fear or nerves, but she secretly felt them when she was a child on her first missions. Artemisa was not a child anymore and in a few hours, she would not be under the slavery of the U.S. government anymore.

Artemisa's leg bounced, she craved her freedom more than anything in life and it was so close. "How long till we land, I need this to be over and I need a drink?" she asked, unable to contain herself much longer. It was bliss to finally ask the question.

Artemisa was informed that they were ready. The power to the property had been cut and it was time. Artemisa led the line, "You've got your assignments, you know the roles you have to play. Let's go kill this dude."

She walked, closely followed by the two commanders as they exited the plane. The security cameras not working meant they could slip through the barbed-wire fence with relative ease.

Artemisa, light on her feet, made her way to the mansion with relative ease, the others thundering around her.

The power being off meant the security on the doors was easy to bypass. Artemisa entered without breaking a sweat and was followed by the commanders hot on her heels.

Artemisa darted through the house, throwing punches at the security team who were investigating the power outage. Artemisa was unconcerned about them as their bodies fell behind her. Her mission was simple: kill Dusk, destroy all his personal computers, cut her tracker out and escape.

She made her way into the study where Dusk was sitting, surrounded by security personnel. Artemisa made quick work of them and soon it was her and Dusk.

Elliot Dusk began to cry as Artemisa stepped over broken legs and dead bodies towards him. "I can pay you, whatever you're being paid I'll double, triple, quadruple."

"You're my ticket to freedom, it's not personal," Artemisa growled, punching him hard in his petrified, sweaty face.

She began destroying the PCs, monitors and laptops. As she was doing this, Artemisa had a thought, and unlocked one of the tablets with Dusk's fingerprints, disabled all security and put the tablet in her backpack. She was curious as to what was so important about this American billionaire which meant he needed to be taken out by the C.I.A.? She trashed the room, and found boxes of cut and uncut emeralds that were ready to be shipped around the world, along with things that no one man should be allowed to afford. Knowing she had minutes before she was joined by the commanders, she shovelled emeralds into her backpack, next to the tablet which was to be her insurance policy.

She took her knife out of her boot. Artemisa felt her lungs expand as she took deep, steadying breaths. She knew what she was about to do and how much it was going to fucking hurt.

'*Think of your freedom*', she thought, as she plunged the knife into her skin.

Air left her lungs as she dug the chip out. Once out, she grabbed the tie from around Dusk's neck and tied it around her arm. Not a moment too soon, as the commanders walked in.

"Mission objective complete," Artemisa announced, "we've got to burn the destroyed equipment and move out."

They nodded at her and began dousing everything in flammable liquid.

She noticed two of the unfamiliar soldiers enter the room behind the commanders, as Artemisa said, "Going to scope the bedroom, make sure there is no more technology."

She left the room and began to walk. As she slid down the laundry chute, she could almost feel how close she was to freedom.

As she came out in the laundry room, Artemisa looked around and saw a woman waiting for her.

"You best be worth the money I am being paid to get you out of here," she muttered, ushering Artemisa towards a car.

"I am," Artemisa said.

"Good," the woman said, fastening her seatbelt and advising Artemisa to do the same. "The eccentric billionaire didn't treat his staff as people; he made us come and go through this tunnel, built so he didn't have to see us."

Artemisa called him a few carefully selected swear words under her breath, but remained silent; she was so close to freedom she couldn't quite believe it, she was so close to being free, but she was also resisting the urge to swear, the pain in her arm throbbing.

They drove in silence for almost two hours, sickness rising with every minute, until the woman turned into a private airport and bid Artemisa good day.

Artemisa walked nervously, looking back at the car which was already pulling away. Her feet felt heavy, her stomach felt like she was going to throw up as she walked in.

"Artemisa, you made good time," a man said to her.

Artemisa looked at him but didn't say anything, just nodding, scared if she opened her mouth, she would be sick on his shoes.

"Hannah sent us. Let's get you away from here." They escorted her to a plane and bid her farewell.

Artemisa looked around suspiciously, but other than the two pilots who greeted her over the intercom, she was alone; she was on her way to freedom.

Artemisa's eyes stung, begging her to close them and rest, but Artemisa shook herself awake or made herself sit in uncomfortable positions in order to stay awake. She was not out of the woods yet and still had reason to be suspicious.

Artemisa tried to occupy her mind by stitching up her arm. It was painful, but it needed to be done sooner rather than later. She didn't do a great job and she knew it would scar once healed.

With this in mind, she jumped to her feet and made her way to the bathroom, looking at her exhausted reflection in the mirror. She took the knife out of her boot, and using the serrated edge of the blade, began to hack off her plaits. Once she had made her way through, she dumped the hair into a bin and went back to her seat.

Artemisa's eyes stung, as the pilot informed her to fasten her seatbelt for landing. She needed to know she was safe and free, she needed to go off on her own.

The plane landed and Artemisa leapt to her feet, grabbed her bag and stood waiting at the plane door, fingers twitching.

Hannah was waiting to greet her, and they ushered Artemisa into a room.

"You're safe," Hannah cried, as the door closed and they wrapped Artemisa in a tight embrace. "You look like fucking shit."

"I feel like fucking shit," Artemisa admitted.

"Let's get down to it then," Hannah said hurriedly. They put a notebook in Artemisa's hand and put a few thousand dollars in cash on the table next to her. "This book is your life, your freedom."

Artemisa opened it, and began flicking through it as Hannah explained. "Bank account details, fake names, I.D. cards, passports."

Artemisa did not know whether it was exhaustion or the

weight of what was happening, but she fought back tears harder than she had fought in South Africa.

"I am free?" she said, unsure whether or not this was actually happening.

"There is a taxi outside, ready to take you wherever," Hannah said, kindly.

"Thank you."

Hannah escorted Artemisa to the taxi, and with one final hug, they let the driver take Artemisa away.

"Where to?" he asked.

Artemisa realised the gravity this question had, she had never had the ability to go wherever she wanted. As the possibilities flew through her mind until exhaustion took over, she said, "A very nice hotel."

He nodded and drove Artemisa in silence the remainder of the way.

Artemisa thanked him and walked into the hotel lobby, and was escorted to a room.

Chapter Three:

Artemisa locked the door, closed the curtains, hid her backpack and got into bed, falling asleep instantly.

Artemisa slept for 17 hours and woke up in a daze. She ordered room service and wondered what she could do, what freedom meant. She spent so much time thinking about this, longing for her freedom and now it was here she didn't know what to do.

She looked at the emeralds and tablet that she had taken from Dusk and thought they would be the most secure in a safety deposit box as opposed to her backpack.

Artemisa walked through the city, the noise was like nothing she had experienced before, or if she had, it had been fleeting. With more cash taken out, emeralds, her file and the tablet secured, Artemisa began exploring New York City.

How far she was walking didn't seem to concern her and it was only when her stomach started to growl, she decided to stop for some food.

Artemisa made it her business over the coming days to explore as much of New York as possible. She took in every tourist attraction that was possible and only returned to the hotel to sleep.

A week after arriving in, Artemisa began to realise that life outside of a military base was very different and she would need to adapt accordingly.

Artemisa crossed the street and to her surprise a man called out to her, "You should smile more."

"You should go fuck yourself," she responded.

The man looked at her with a startled look on his face, as Artemisa glared at him before he eventually walked on.

'The fucking nerve on that guy', she thought as she walked on, eventually stopping at a bar for a drink, the sheer amount of people and the noise of the city crushing her mind.

If Artemisa wanted a quiet evening drink, however, she was not going to get it.

"Can I buy you a drink?" a voice asked her from behind.

She turned to see a man, old enough to be her father, leering at her.

"No thank you, I can buy my own drinks," Artemisa said politely.

"No, my treat. I'll buy you a drink."

"No, thank you," Artemisa repeated, a lot less politely.

"Don't be like that, I'll buy you one."

"Ask me again and I'll fucking bottle you," Artemisa said loudly, getting up from the stool and facing the man, her full bottle of beer in her hand.

"Easy, easy," the bartender huffed, encouraging Artemisa to take her seat and clearing the old man away from her.

Artemisa scowled at her drink and sat in silence, despite the bartender offering her multiple apologies.

It took a while for Artemisa to calm down and stop seeking a fight with every man who came to the bar or called her sweetheart that evening, and she went back to the hotel in a foul mood.

This foul mood didn't disappear overnight and Artemisa awoke early and headed to the hotel gym for a vigorous workout, in an attempt to calm the storm inside her mind. It did not work.

So Artemisa decided to walk around the city and see what trouble she could cause. Nothing got her out of a bad mood like her fists connecting with some arsehole's face.

Artemisa didn't find any trouble, try as she might, which did nothing to improve her mood. She was just thinking about where to go for lunch, a voice behind her made her stomach sink as she readied herself for a fight. "Artemisa, is that you? We've been searching New York for you."

Artemisa turned to see who had spoken, to see a man, a little shorter than her, a thin pencil moustache and hair combed over, a combination of silver grey and jet black.

"A friend sent us, Richard Cherry," he explained, as Artemisa began looking for her get-out options. "Allow me to buy you lunch and I'll explain why Richard sent me."

"How do I know Richard sent you?" she asked, still ready for a fight.

"He said you might be bored with the music on the MP3 player he gave you and thought I could help, broaden your horizon, help with how overwhelming the city is."

Artemisa unclenched her fists and said, "Fine, lunch but no guarantees."

"Excellent, how does Italian sound?"

"If you're paying it sounds excellent," Artemisa said, cautiously.

He held a door open for her, from a car on the kerb and a driver took them both to an Italian restaurant.

He held the door open for her and they walked to a seat.

"Order whatever you like, it's on me."

"Double whiskey and cola, and you can tell me how you know Richard Cherry, and why you know who I am and why I exist," Artemisa said.

"I have worked with Richard Cherry in the past."

"And you are?"

"Roman Magaldi."

"Why did he contact you about me?"

"He did not explain much about you, only that you have not had much of a life and that I could help give you some of that back."

"How?" Artemisa said, accepting the drink from the

waiter who brought it over.

"I own a number of businesses in New York. A cinema, tattoo parlours, a casino, a bar, a music venue, waste management companies, things like that. I would like to pay you to watch films in the cinema, catch-up on things you've missed, if you want to explore New York, I would like to pay you to do that. If you decide you want tattoos, I would like to pay you to do that. A mutually beneficial agreement. I can provide you with a place to live as well. I also have friends who have similar businesses across the city, where you can also spend your time at a greatly discounted price."

"How does you paying me to sit in the cinema help you?" Artemisa said curiously, sensing where the conversation was going.

"The cinema I own takes a number of private bookings, people can book out a screen. These bookings can be either cash or card, they can be put down as business expenses."

"So, I get to spend months watching movies, going to music gigs, sitting in bars, things I have been deprived of and you get to *balance the books?*" Artemisa asked.

"Exactly."

"What do you recommend off the menu?" Artemisa asked, mulling the proposal over.

"Any of the linguini dishes," he said.

Artemisa ordered the same as Roman Magaldi. As they waited for the food to be prepared, Artemisa decided to quiz the Italian sat opposite her a bit more. "So tell me about your business ventures?"

"I am a simple man, trying to provide the best possible life for my family."

"You have children?"

"No, my wife passed. Four winters ago. I have a mother, brothers, sisters, nieces, nephews, who I love dearly. I want the best life for them."

"Do they all live in New York?"

"Some do, some live in Chicago. You are very inquisitive."

"I have just left the employment of the U.S. government, which was not a job I wished to have. If I am to be employed again, I want to know exactly who I am working for."

"Understandable, it is important you have the freedom to choose what you want to do, that is why Richard pointed me in your direction. A few films a day or a week, it is entirely at your leisure, should you take the job."

"A cinema, tattoo parlours, waste management, a casino. You certainly have a broad horizon."

"I am an ambitious man; I want to run the best business in New York, and to do that I need to know how to run a variety of different businesses, cash in hand, small companies, large companies. All to know how my employees benefit. Even an Italian restaurant or two, because my people deserve to only eat the best."

Artemisa was growing weary of beating around the bush. She was sitting opposite the leader of a mafia, and she wanted him to admit it and start this off with honesty. If she wanted to catch-up on movies, she could do that without needing to be in the employment of the mafia.

"That is, of course, the side of the business which you need to concern yourself with," he said, as the linguini was put down in front of them.

"So, there is another side?"

"There is, but as I say, you do not need to be concerned with it, that work is not what I am looking to employ you for."

Artemisa nodded slowly, "So you want me to watch movies, eat Italian?"

"Essentially. However, if you want to explore other businesses, you are welcome to."

"You mentioned a place to live as well?" Artemisa said, recalling the conversation.

"Naturally. As I said, I treat my employees well."

Artemisa mulled this over, an uneasy feeling in her stomach that was nothing to do with the proposal that had just been presented before her. She collected her thoughts and said, "Allow me a few days to think it over and tell me where I can find our mutual friend, Mr Cherry."

Roman Magaldi nodded and instructed one of the people around him to get Artemisa a flip phone. Once it was in Artemisa's pocket, Roman Magaldi said to her, "I will let you know his location and you can let me know your answer."

Artemisa thanked him for the meal and the proposal and left. She walked cautiously, ensuring she was not being followed by any of Magaldi's men before she got on the subway back towards the hotel.

As the subway train trundled down the tracks, it illuminated one of the many things Artemisa had been made unaware of by living exclusively on military bases, and it was the commonplace sexual harassment of women. Artemisa took off her headphones, as she noticed four men leering at a woman across from them.

Artemisa had heard enough, when one of them complimented the woman's breasts. She got up calmly and sat next to the woman. Artemisa then leant across the aisle and took the knife out of her boot.

"If you ever leer or give a woman an unwanted sexual comment again, you'll never wake up," Artemisa vowed, in a voice so sweet it was dangerous.

The men weren't sure how to respond to this. They didn't see the knife, as Artemisa held it up her sleeve.

"Now I suggest you fuck off down the other end of the train before I start smashing skulls in," Artemisa warned them.

They took her advice and scurried off.

"Thank you," the woman whispered.

"You're welcome," Artemisa said, offering her the penknife.

"I have spray in my bag, thank you," she politely declined the offer.

"What stop are you getting off at? Do you need me to stay with you?" Artemisa asked.

"Only three more, thankfully."

Artemisa felt her phone vibrate in her pocket but ignored it. Her main focus was ensuring the girl got off at her stop okay. Artemisa escorted her off the train onto the platform, before sitting down and locking eyes with the men who were still on the subway. She had never been prepared for society to be like this and it filled her with a rage she couldn't begin to describe.

When Artemisa finally closed the door to her hotel room, she had a text from Roman Magaldi with the details and contact number for Richard Cherry.

This improved her mood by the smallest modicum. She messaged him with a time and place to meet him tomorrow morning and she fell onto the bed in a foul mood; too many thoughts in her head to ever hope for a good night's sleep.

Artemisa gave it up as a bad job and headed down to the hotel gym to kill time, before she killed Richard Cherry.

Artemia's queasy feeling was matched with the incandescent rage she had towards Richard Cherry, as she walked a semi-familiar path to the Irish bar she had been to the other night. Artemisa didn't know whether he would actually show but she hoped for his sake he did; she was not much in the mood for burning the entire city to smoke him out of wherever he was.

She took a seat in a darkened corner booth; hood up, eyes narrowed, waiting and watching. The pub was quiet but for an old couple at the bar and some tourists who were having a cooked breakfast.

Artemisa sat, leg bouncing, anger bubbling and a stony look on her face, for 45 minutes, until Richard Cherry walked into the pub and towards her booth.

Artemisa's stony look turned into a scowl, brow furrowed; she didn't reply in greeting as he sat down.

"What is with that look?" he asked.

If Artemisa wasn't so angry, she would be impressed with how someone so moronic could have gotten so far in life.

She took a few moments to compose herself before saying, "Not only did you tell someone I existed, that I was alive, YOU told a goddamn fucking mob boss."

Richard Cherry let out a sigh before, "Firstly, Artemisa, I don't think Mr Magaldi would be happy with you referring to him as such and secondly, I did not tell him what you could do, simply that you had a childhood ripped away from you and that you could benefit from his owning of a cinema complex. I invested far too much into getting you out of there alive to go blabbing about you."

"Your word means very little to me right now," Artemisa scowled, resisting the urge to kill the man right here in the booth. "Unlock all security on your phone and hand it over."

Richard Cherry obliged her and handed over his phone. Artemisa began scrolling through and he ordered them both a drink, completely at ease as if it were a normal thing. Once Artemisa was satisfied, she formulated a plan and gave him his phone back.

"See, nothing to worry about."

Artemisa nodded and drained her nearly full pint before saying, "I need to check a few things with you, about South Africa. Let's take a walk."

Richard Cherry nodded and followed, leaving his full pint behind. Artemisa asked him benign questions about the mission, and the lies that were told to the media about the nature of the incident, until they reached a busy crossroad.

Artemisa kept her breathing calm as she scouted her opportunity. They joined a gaggle of people waiting to cross the busy street. They jostled about as Artemisa separated herself from Richard Cherry. She saw her moment and took it, clutching his hand and squeezing it until she knew that he was dead; she then created a domino effect, knocking the person next person in line so eventually Richard Cherry's body fell into the road and the path of a lorry carrying electronic goods, which could not brake in time.

Artemisa was already walking off, not stopping to watch what was about to unfold. She made her way back to her hotel, a weight off her shoulders and a clarity in her mind, now she had been through Richard Cherry's mobile.

Back in the hotel gym, Artemisa began weighing up the pros and cons of taking this job with Roman Magaldi. There weren't really any negatives; if Magaldi kept to his word then she wouldn't need to get involved in the other sides of his business, nor did she want to.

Artemisa made a concerted effort, as she idly scrolled through the hotel TV, to vow to herself that if Magaldi wanted her to get involved and start killing, then she would walk away from him and his business dealing, but for the meantime it couldn't hurt rinsing him for all he was worth and enjoy his very generous hospitality and from the sounds of it, the generosity of other mafia families in New York.

Artemisa rang him the next morning and he invited her for a morning coffee. Artemisa didn't drink coffee, but she accepted the offer. She dressed and headed to the location, with a knot in her stomach that she couldn't quite untie.

Artemisa was suspicious at how warmly Roman Magaldi greeted her, but she reasoned that this was more due to how she had previously been treated than anything else.

Roman Magaldi had his assistant hand Artemisa a key and delicately handwritten directions to her new apartment.

"I have had the liberty of having everything that Mr Magaldi owns listed in your home," the assistant said, in a warm voice. "So you can experience New York and live in New York the Magaldi way."

"Thank you," Artemisa said awkwardly, accepting the key and the directions.

"This is from me," Roman Magaldi said, and he slid across the table a golden coin, the size of her palm.

This piqued Artemisa's curiosity, she picked it up and examined it. It was intricately designed and Artemisa looked over the coin after a while to meet Roman Magaldi's eyes, as she could tell he was looking forward to explaining what the inconveniently sized coin represented.

"Show this coin at any of the Magaldi establishments or an establishment owned by an associate, and they will know you are a part of our family, and you can get the rewards that come with that. It will ensure that you are not confused with the common folk and get you the discount, respect and privacy you are entitled to."

"Thank you," Artemisa said again, holding the coin in both of her hands.

"Would you like us to drive you to the apartment or would you prefer to walk?"

"I will walk if it's all the same to you? I am still trying to get familiar with the city."

"It is a big city," he chuckled.

Artemisa excused herself from the table, leaving the cup of coffee untouched, and headed in the direction of the subway station. She spent the day collecting her things from the hotel, before following the directions given to her by Mr Magaldi's assistant.

She was greeted by the concierge, who escorted her up in the lift to her new apartment and bid her a good evening as he returned downstairs.

Artemisa stood awkwardly in the doorway to this fully furnished apartment and looked around. She didn't quite know what to do with herself, having never really had a place with such privacy and such a warm feeling.

Artemisa really wanted to feel like she would not be betrayed and she was safe, but despite this feeling she couldn't ignore her training, and went round the apartment checking for bugs, or planted cameras. After the apartment passed her inspection, she took a beer out of the fridge and sat on the couch, TV remote in hand, wondering if this is what normal people did.

Artemisa found herself enjoying New York a lot more now she knew the city as well as any of the military bases she had spent time in; she knew the best places to eat, the best places to drink, the best places for a fight if she wanted to let off some steam. Artemisa also knew the seedy side of New York incredibly well; she knew where the politicians would go to if they wanted to do all manner of unspeakable acts of varying degrees of illegality, she knew the best places to dispose of a body, where to hide anything from counterfeit money to legitimate money that had not been put into bank accounts. She knew everything about Magaldi's operation despite her best intentions not to get involved in the mafia. Artemisa couldn't help but be an exceptional eavesdropper, when she was too young to kill, Artemisa was used by the military for this purpose.

People had obviously been told about Artemisa, as they welcomed her warmly and greeted her as if they had been lifelong friends. What they had been told about her, concerned her slightly. They were openly hostile about the U.S. military, which either meant they watched the news, understood history or they were trying to get on her good side. Nobody seemed very concerned about hiding what they did around her as well and from what she could gather, Mr Magaldi had no understanding as to what she could do; they all seemed to keep their distance.

Artemisa couldn't believe it had only been four weeks since she had killed Richard Cherry. Artemisa was settling into New York life nicely and that day she had a whole movie screen booked, just for her, so she could watch some of the *'modern classics'* she had missed out on.

The staff in the cinema were all exceptionally nice to her, ensuring she had enough popcorn and drinks to last her the entire movie and explaining what made certain movies so great.

Artemisa made her way through the city, one earphone in and one ear listening to the sound of traffic. Artemisa learned very quickly not to be too distracted when navigating the city or she would be run over; not something she was keen on doing, it would rather upset things.

The coin that Mr Magaldi had given her was more valuable than she previously realised. She paid pennies in restaurants, had V.I.P. access into some of the most exclusive places in New York and everybody treated her like royalty inside those places. And although she saw her fair share of fights, disagreements and gang brawls whenever she ventured to a different location, she had not gotten involved once and was quite proud of herself.

Chapter Four:

After four months in New York, Artemisa didn't realise how much her life had changed, until she realised she was drinking cocktails at midday with a news reporter from one of the local channels at the next table, whose dazzling smile kept pulling Artemisa's attention away from the book she was reading.

Artemisa forgot that the drinking age in the U.S.A. was 21, since her captors realised that if she was tipsy or drunk, she was less likely to kill random troops, until she saw one of the people in the bar looking at her with an inquisitive expression and muttering to those they were with.

If there was one thing Artemisa disliked about New York, it was how much she was bothered. These fuckwits seemed to think it was impossible for anyone to enjoy their own company, so she was constantly having to deal with people coming over, offering to buy her a drink or trying to engage her in conversation. Even when she had both earphones in and a book in front of her, she still seemed to get bothered.

Artemisa was regretting her lunch choice as the muttering continued. She never had people look at her like this when she went to the 'Rye Curious Whiskey Bar'; in fact, everyone was so nice to her in there, the bartenders and patrons greeted her brightly whenever she entered and engaged her in conversation when she was in the mood for it and let her be when she was not.

The man who was looking at her was making his way over and Artemisa let out a sigh.

"Is this seat taken?" the man asked her, indicating the seat opposite her.

Artemisa was slightly relieved it was not someone coming over to question her age, just to annoy the shit out of her. "If it was taken, there would be someone in it, if I wanted someone in it, then there would be someone in it," Artemisa explained casually.

"I mean no offence, I was just curious about the book you were reading."

Artemisa looked down at the table where a book on philosophy sat.

"There is a bookstore about two blocks east," Artemisa said, as politely as possible, as if she welcomed her peace being interrupted.

"May I ask how old you are? You look young, younger than 21," he snapped, his tone changing.

"May I ask if you have had any plastic surgery?" Artemisa responded.

"I… I have not," he replied, evidently confused.

"Is it something you have considered?"

"No, I don't think so."

"Well then, I'm 30 seconds away from my glass making a

connection with your face. I will carve it up so badly they'll need to reconstruct your face from scratch. So unless you want that to happen then leave me in peace." Artemisa raised her voice at this, so more tables could hear.

The news reporter chuckled at this, and the man slunk away.

Artemisa sighed deeply and drained her glass. She went over to make a comment about the man to the floor manager, before returning to collect her things; she was running late for her appointment. As Artemisa packed her books, she noticed the news reporter's card sticking out of a corner.

Artemisa privately thought that her file, the tablet and all of her secrets would make a good news story, should she ever need the leverage, but then again Artemisa might ring her number just to look at her smile again.

Artemisa walked four blocks, until she arrived outside one of the few Mr Magaldi businesses she had not visited: a tattoo parlour. Artemisa had been thinking about designs for the past few months, and with a few hidden details that only she would be able to understand, meant she would not need to walk around carrying all the bank details for all of her different accounts which had caused a few questions.

Artemisa was excited to discuss the designs and was thankful that everyone in the parlour were under the employment of Mr Magaldi, it made her life more peaceful.

For a mafia boss, Artemisa saw Mr Magaldi more often than she initially expected. Whenever she did, he invited her over or sat with her, talking to her at length about his day, never asking for her to comment or express an opinion, but just as someone to listen to.

Artemisa secretly thought he liked someone who wasn't going to kiss his arse and suck up to him. She saw him about twice a month, if she had to average it, and if she was being honest with herself, it was quite nice having him talk whilst also valuing the fact she was introverted and liked to keep things simple. He was more open with her now, discussing his empire at length and the struggles he faced, when he faced them.

One evening, when he joined her for a drink before her meal arrived, he said, "Artemisa, now that you have been here a few months, I have learnt a lot about you. However, in the Magaldi family, we like to celebrate! We are Italian, so we need to know your birthday! So please enlighten me."

Artemisa sat deep in thought, trying to remember if her file, currently locked in a safety deposit box, even had the answer to this question. The longer she thought, she was not sure if it even had her birth date on it. "I... I don't know it," Artemisa said honestly. "I decided on the date of the 8th July, but it never really made a difference to me."

"So why that date? Why July 8th?"

"Somebody decided to name me after Artemisia Lomi Gentileschi, the Italian Renaissance painter. Maybe they liked her depictions of death, maybe they knew my work would be overshadowed by men for far too long. I don't know, all I know is I was given a first name by an unknown individual. So I adopted her birthday as mine, as I never really knew my own birthday. It seemed fitting."

"Well as long as you are happy with your name then we need to celebrate your birthday!"

"Thank you," Artemisa said awkwardly.

"Now, I have business to take care of and you have a book to dive into," he said, tapping his knuckles on the cover of the book next to her, "I shall leave you for now."

"I hope business goes well for you, Mr Magaldi," Artemisa replied respectfully.

Once Artemisa had eaten her fill of the chef's superb cooking, she made her way back to her apartment. She was cautious to not trust Mr Magaldi, given the fact he was the head of a mafia family, but also had to reason that he was treating her well and sticking to his word about her involvement in his more illegal activities.

The next week, Artemisa slung on a t-shirt and hoodie and made her way towards the tattoo parlour. This was the day that she had been waiting for and was the first time she was making a decision about her body.

Artemisa sat down with a cup of tea, as Amy began

discussing the designs and putting the stencils on Artemisa's arm.

"How do you cope with pain?" Amy asked as she positioned her.

"I think I'll be alright," Artemisa smirked at her.

"Well if not, I'll pin you down. This piece will take a while so if you need a break just let me know," Amy said, switching on the television in the corner and handing Artemisa the remote.

Artemisa thought about her reply to this, but as the needle pierced her skin for the first time, she kept the reply to herself.

The next few days were long. Artemisa sat in the chair for three days in a row, watching the television and listening to Amy tell her stories about her work. Amy liked to talk as she worked and she also liked to reassure Artemisa about how well she was doing as the needle broke her skin, minute after minute, hour after hour, day after day.

Artemisa was thrilled with the work, but despite Amy's suggestion of coming back in to start the second arm, Artemisa decided to wait a few months before accepting her offer.

Chapter Five:

"I must say, they did beautiful work," Mr Magaldi said, causing Artemisa to jump up from her book and almost knocking over her drink.

"I didn't see you," Artemisa said, shifting everything in front of her so that he could sit across from her, She did not expect to see him in the bar she was in at this time of the day.

"I'm sorry to have startled you," he said, taking a seat.

Artemisa looked around, and for the first time she noticed he was alone, which was strange, but she paid it no heed as he ordered a drink.

"How are you feeling, now you've been here for a couple of months?"

Artemisa pondered this question for a while before saying, "I.. I am content, I feel normal, which is very good!"

"Excellent, I am glad to hear this. Is there anything you need?"

"Not that I can think of."

"Well if there is, make sure you come to me."

"Thank you."

Mr Magaldi left Artemisa to her own devices. As she reopened her book, she thought it was nice that he was checking in on her.

Weeks turned to months and life was quiet. Artemisa spent her time enjoying New York. She would work out when she pleased, she watched films when she wanted, drank where she wanted, ate where she wanted and explored at her leisure. Mr Magaldi was sure to sit with her and hear all about what she had been up to, and use Artemisa's ears to drone on about the highs and lows of running a mafia.

One evening, when walking into a bar, Artemisa was surprised to find a bottle of champagne waiting for her, to celebrate one year as part of the Magaldi family, as she ventured into one of her usual go-to spots.

One Thursday, Artemisa noticed Mr Magaldi enter the restaurant, and for the first time she could remember he looked stressed as he sat opposite her.

"Is something the matter, Mr Magaldi?" Artemisa asked politely.

"It is my assistant and driver, Alexander," he sighed. "He is in a state."

"How come?"

"His wife has just gone into labour. Earlier than expected. Midwife is confident that both mother and baby will be fine, he is nervous."

"Is he at the hospital with them now?"

"Yes, he is there now, and he will go on paternity leave," Mr Magaldi said.

"Be sure to send them my best?" Artemisa said, unsure of how to lead this conversation, having no experience with babies.

"Sorry to burden this with you, my dear. We were still looking for someone to replace Alexander with weeks to spare, but now…" He paused, looking off into the distance.

"What were the activities that Alexander oversaw?" Artemisa asked.

"Drive me to the office in the morning, depending on where I wanted lunch, he would drive me to lunch, if I needed to drop something off at a business I own, then he would drop it off," Mr Magaldi explained.

Artemisa privately thought that a driver would be easy to find, until Mr Magaldi said, "The most important thing is that he never listened to the conversations I had."

There was a long pause here, as Mr Magaldi muttered in Italian and swilled the wine in his glass, thinking hard.

Artemisa empathised with his struggle but sat in silence, not knowing what she could really offer.

"Artemisa, my darling. Would you do me the biggest favour, just for a few weeks, if it is not too much trouble. I know you would not listen or pay attention to me in the back of the car, and it wouldn't be too strenuous."

Artemisa looked at the man opposite her and thought about the question that had just been posed. If it was nothing illegal, then why not? After all, he had been checking in on her a lot.

"I can sit in the driver's seat of a car, go from location A to location B and only pay attention to the road."

Mr Magaldi let out a cry of relief and thanked her profusely.

The next morning, Artemisa put on a suit, picked up the keys to an expensive SUV, and entered Mr Magaldi's address into the satnav.

The car was an automatic, so Artemisa put the radio on and made good time. She got out of the car to hold the door open for Mr Magaldi.

After telling Artemisa where to go, Mr Magaldi kept singing her praises and telling her how grateful he was for her assistance.

Artemisa sat in the car reading her book and listening to music until it was time to drive Mr Magaldi to the next location. Artemisa had to say, it wasn't too much of a change from her normal day-to-day activities.

As Artemisa sat, she realised that it must be coming up to a year since she had killed anyone, a feat that she wouldn't have thought possible.

Artemisa tried her best to not pay attention to Mr Magaldi whilst taking calls in the car, but it was inevitable.

She listened to him talk in depth about drugs, money laundering, the role Artemisa and a few others played in this, cops and politicians that needed to be paid off, and opposition to his taking control of the city.

Artemisa paid no attention, did not speak her mind or voice an opinion on anything until about five weeks later, when Mr. Magaldi was on the phone, regarding his own safety.

"I'll be lucky if I see out the year if things like this keep happening, pay off whoever we need to in order to keep the heat down and start investigating if we have a snitch."

Artemisa realised that her heavily subsidised lifestyle would change if her boss was murdered, so as his conversation continued, she began making the tactical calculations.

When he was off that call, she said, "Mr Magaldi, that call, I couldn't help overhearing, is there a threat on your life?"

"Potentially, a business rival has been making some decisions that may impact me in the future."

"If I may, when under my previous employment I got into a lot of houses and a lot of places that I was not meant to be. Your house is problematic. If you would like I could offer some alternatives and point out some weaknesses."

"That would be very kind of you Artemisa, I will take you up on that."

That evening, Artemisa sat with a drink in her hand with

Mr Magaldi and some of his associates, whom he did not introduce as they were there to just listen and take notes.

"So, darling Artemisa, please bestow your knowledge on us."

"Firstly, the location of your home, as lovely as it is, is isolated. If you were in trouble, the soonest anyone could get to your house would be maybe a 10,15 minute drive, traffic permitting. In a house, the only staff you could have on site would be limited and impact your convenience, not to mention your privacy."

"So what would you suggest?" Mr. Magaldi said, listening intently.

"Move into the city. Top floor penthouse, that way you can have as many people as you need in the skyscraper, rent out the other spaces to make money. Plus, in the city you can have someone with a sniper rifle on every rooftop if you need them within minutes, reinforced glass to keep you safe. In a penthouse apartment, someone killing you would have one way in, one way out, you can implement different things to ensure your safety. You being wiser, would have other escape options that coupled with security, and lockdown procedures in place."

"Interesting."

"So move into a penthouse apartment, reinforce the glass, install a private elevator or a panic room, implement security measures and protocols, and consolidate as many people that you need in the building as and when the situation calls for it," Artemisa summarised.

"Go over the defence advantages of a penthouse again, please?" one of the people behind Mr Magaldi said.

"When you're in a penthouse, there is one way in, one way out: the front door. Private elevators may be two ways in or out. At most three, if you account for a full building fire evacuation, meaning an assassin, for example, would have one way in or one way out to get to the penthouse. If in danger, you could have men in every room on every floor, so that if someone just walks in and starts shooting their way up, floor by floor, they would be dead before they got close. Even if they did have snipers on the roof opposite for protection, all whilst you pour yourself a wine, sit in a panic room until it is all over and then you continue with your day," Artemisa explained.

When they nodded but did not say anything, Artemisa continued by saying, "In the middle of the city you can call back-up in, call the cops, call whoever and they will get there a lot quicker," Artemisa explained, as if she were speaking to a toddler.

"I like the idea," Mr Magaldi said after a long pause, "Artemisa, is there a building in the U.S.A. you could not get into?"

"With the right resources, time and people who weren't fucking idiots-"

"Language!"

"Sorry, with the right resources, time and people I reckon I could get into any building," Artemisa said modestly.

"If I gave you the right resources, time and people... could you take up the task of making a building so secure you could not venture into it, regardless of the time, people and resources?"

"I'll think of ideas, if you find me a building."

Mr Magaldi let out cries of relief and thanks, as Artemisa drained the rest of her glass and bid them all goodnight.

As Artemisa walked through the New York night, she paused to scream profanities before heading back home.

Artemisa slammed the door to her flat and began to pace the living room furiously, only stopping to swear while she had an angry argument with herself for volunteering the information. When she accepted Mr Magaldi's offer, she was to sit in the cinema and watch films and allow him to act in the background, doing whatever he needed to do, and now she was helping him establish an impenetrable fortress in New York.

She had made the calculated decision to volunteer the information to keep up her comfortable lifestyle, but she had not meant to oversee the construction of it herself and now she was in the thick of his operations.

As Artemisa tried to steady her breathing, she made a decision to not reveal her full hand and create Mr Magaldi's new business hub to be impenetrable to anyone not named Artemisa, as an insurance policy, and then she was out, done.

Artemisa slept badly that night, she tossed and turned before giving it up as a bad job. She couldn't shake the feeling she was playing a dangerous game, offering her expertise to Mr Magaldi, as it may encourage him to ask more leading questions about her past, and given what Richard Cherry might have exposed about her, she didn't want Mr Magaldi making any more use out of her skills.

Artemisa shook more than she had in a long time as she sat, waiting for Mr. Magaldi; her leg bounced, her fingers tapped the steering wheel and she had a million thoughts running through her head at a million miles per hour.

Mr Magaldi entered the car, startling Artemisa before he instructed her to drive.

"Where are we heading?"

"Club Cinnamon."

"Understood."

Artemisa parked up but rather than waiting for Mr Magaldi in the car, he requested she accompany him. She followed at a distance, wondering why she was following him.

Mr Cinnamon and Mr Magaldi greeted each other and as they sat, Artemisa was brought a glass of whiskey as she stood listening to their meeting, despite not ordering it or hearing Mr Magaldi order anything, although he had a glass of wine in his hand.

Mr Cinnamon was a fence by the sounds of it, as he and Mr Magaldi discussed the movement of various types of merchandise. Artemisa grew bored of the conversation very quickly but listened to every word, making a mental note of everything that was being said.

When the meeting was finally over, Mr Magaldi waited in the car before giving Artemisa her instructions on where to take him, then eventually advising her to take him home.

When Artemisa pulled up in the driveway however, he instructed her to follow him. He unlocked a door directly into an office, where Artemisa saw the same people who had sat behind Mr Magaldi when Artemisa had offered up her ideas.

"I believe it is time I make some introductions," Mr Magaldi explained.

"Artemisa, this is Nicoletta Cosma, my personal lawyer." He indicated the woman who was staring daggers at her. Artemisa gave the smug-looking woman a once over as Mr Magaldi continued.

"Hi," Artemisa said, returning the lack of a smile.

"Tony the Barber, my Head of Security," indicating the bald giant in an expensive suit, who was squeezed into a chair at the other side of the desk.

"A pleasure," Artemisa said, as Tony at least gave her a

small smile.

"These are the two who have helped me create my business empire and now they are the ones who will work under you, as you help me resolve the small issue of staying alive, so that the empire will flourish."

Neither of them seemed best pleased with the fact that they would be working under Artemisa, and Artemisa could understand why. However, she had a job to do, and she would do it.

Over the coming days, Artemisa found it strange to be giving orders and having them followed. They asked her about bullet-resistant glass, and after getting her recommendations on the different types and the benefits, they eventually found the right companies for the job, and made contact to discuss installations. As they worked together in the same room, Artemisa asked more questions than she had in the past year, wanting to know about the people she was working with.

Artemisa spent her time researching companies to install a private elevator as well as a failsafe system. It took six days of research until Artemisa found the company that ticked every box. She made her appointment, instructed Nicoletta and Tony what she needed them to be doing whilst she was away, and began to drive.

As Head of Security, Tony wanted to come with her, but Artemisa declined firmly and gave him a complex task that had no real bearing on anything, but knew would be time-consuming.

Artemisa felt liberated over the long drive, she had her music playing loud and the traffic was light. Artemisa made good time as she pulled into the industrial estate; she realised she was 20 minutes early as she parked up and walked into the building.

"Hi, can we help you?" a receptionist asked, with a tone that Artemisa had disturbed him greatly, as he glanced up from the computer in front of them.

"I have an appointment," Artemisa said.

"Take a seat," he instructed.

Artemisa did not take a seat. Instead, she stood, fingers tapping, impatience growing as they kept her waiting. She had a role to play and did her best to let them know she was important.

Finally, a man came walking towards her with a jolly spring in his step, not at all apologetic that they had kept her waiting.

"Ah you must be my next appointment, you're early."

"My appointment was fifteen minutes ago," Artemisa replied.

"My apologies. I'm Gareth Elis, CEO. Follow me, let's talk business."

Artemisa followed him into his office before he took a

seat behind the desk.

"So, there weren't too many details given over the phone. Please, tell us what we can do for you."

"I am here on behalf of my employer, Roman Magaldi," Artemisa explained.

As she said his name, she could see fear flicker in his eyes and beads of sweat start to form on his forehead. "I am overseeing the building of Mr Magaldi's new penthouse, I am looking to build him a secure room."

"I understand."

"I want the door to have iris, fingerprint, pin, and key security. The keys will be kept here until asked for them, the pin and fingerprint will be set up by Mr Magaldi himself. I will be the omega level access with my iris scan, and only mine. We will also be requiring multiple non-disclosure agreements taken out on every level of security."

"Ah, I see you have done your research."

"Obviously," Artemisa muttered, "the secure room, panic room, safe room, call it what you will, could you build one that is also an elevator, if I co-ordinate everything with the technicians who are building and installing it?"

Gareth Elis thought about this for a few minutes before he eventually said, "Yes, we could do that, install metrics at the bottom, as well as to the safe room. Yes, we could."

"Excellent. Let us begin."

"Excuse me?" he fumbled.

"I want the omega level authorisation setup now; I want to then set up Mr Magaldi's fingerprint and pin, and then construction to begin."

"We will need to work with our design technicians."

"Good, let's get started," Artemisa interjected, reaching into her pocket and taking out a mobile phone. "The architect has put the blueprints and floorplans on this. I don't know how they work but it should be easy to find, as well as the contact details for the people you'll need to co-ordinate with."

Artemisa stretched back in her chair, as Gareth Elis sweated behind his desk. This was not how he was expecting the meeting to go, but as it was most convenient for Artemisa, she did not allow him to dictate how the meeting would go.

"I have everything I need," he eventually said, after 45 minutes.

"Excellent."

Artemisa stayed in her seat as he consulted with various different people via his laptop, and he and the design experts worked everything out.

"I will need you to sign all of the necessary paperwork," he said, placing several documents in front of her, his sweat staining the paper.

Artemisa read and signed everything, separated the paperwork containing the non-disclosure agreement between herself and the company regarding her OMEGA level clearance, and arranged a date for Mr Magaldi to set up his own security.

"Pleasure doing business with you. The Magaldi family is pleased with the speed and discretion with which you conduct business," Artemisa said, leaving with a laptop to set up Mr Magaldi's fingerprints.

"Thank you," Gareth Elis said breathlessly.

Artemisa left the facility with a smug look on her face, and when she got into the car, paperwork in the passenger seat next to her, she laughed. It was fun knowing she had secrets about Mr Magaldi.

Before calling it a day, she stopped at the bank to put her non-disclosure agreement in her safety deposit box, before heading to the Rye Curious Whiskey Bar.

Although not a place where she got her Magaldi discount, Artemisa enjoyed her time there and never got bothered by strangers or by men.

She ordered a drink and sat down, letting out a sigh. She couldn't shake a claustrophobic feeling, so Artemisa got up and sat somewhere with her back against a wall and the rest of the bar in her eyeline.

As Artemisa went for a refill, a girl she had seen regularly over the past year said, "Not seen you in a suit before, it suits you."

"Thank you," Artemisa said, awkwardly, "I don't really wear suits."

"You should," she smiled, her eyes looking Artemisa up and down, before collecting her drink and walking away.

This cheered Artemisa up, as she sat collecting her thoughts over a few drinks before eventually heading back for the evening.

The next few days were a whirlwind of planning meetings, construction meetings and briefing those who worked for Mr Magaldi. This provided Artemisa with complete access to all of Mr Magaldi's records, which in turn provided Artemisa with complete knowledge of every aspect of Mr Magaldi's businesses, both legal and illegal. She had no way of keeping any of the information, but she wrote down what she could and stored the scraps of paper around her body, before putting them in her deposit box that evening.

Within four months, the weather started to turn and Artemisa found herself having to defrost the car windscreen before doing anything.

One morning, after providing a drop for Mr Magaldi, she parked the car in a locked area of the below-ground car parking, which led to the safe room. The build was coming along nicely and Artemisa would be relieved when it was finished. She was sleeping less and her emotional state was slipping closer to what it had been like when she was with the C.I.A. and the U.S. military.

This gave Artemisa unpleasant memories of all of her previous missions, in particular South Africa. Artemisa wondered, if she had gone back in time to South Africa and told her past self she would be running a mafia on behalf of someone else, how she would have reacted to this.

It hadn't escaped Artemisa's notice that Mr Magaldi was asking her for advice on what was quintessentially a power grab over the dominant mafia families in New York, and whatever Artemisa suggested was seemingly being implemented.

'You haven't been in a cinema room for months', a voice at the back of her mind kept saying to her whenever she found herself in these situations.

Artemisa now no longer wanted anything to do with Mr Magaldi, and yet she found herself working longer hours, strategically planning his monopolisation of New York.

One day, some months later, Artemisa decided, as a coping mechanism for the stress, to book in with the hairdresser. As Artemisa spent hours looking at her reflection, she did as she did when she first spoke to Mr Magaldi - weighed up the pros and cons. Now she was determined. She would leave his employment.

How did one leave the employment of a mafia boss? This was the question she pondered on as she walked through the city.

As Artemisa considered this she looked up at the sky, and despite just having her hair done, Artemisa dug a hat and scarf out of her bag as the first few snowflakes of winter began to fall. If she didn't meet Mr Magaldi now, she never would. His penthouse was secure and having furniture moved in. She had provided more than enough information as to how to end the competition. She wanted out, and as the snow began to fall thick and fast, she wanted somewhere warm as well.

Artemisa shook the snow off her jacket as she stepped into the foyer of Magaldi's new central hub. She inserted her key into the lift and made her way up to Mr Magaldi's new property.

As she got out of the lift, she was greeted by Tony, towering above her and not at all happy that she was there.

"We thought you were not working today," he said to her bluntly.

"Careful, Tony, you still work for me," Artemisa said with a forced chuckle. "Relax, big lad. I am just here to check a few things and then have a private word with the boss."

"Mr Magaldi is in a meeting," Tony grunted, before turning and heading towards the office.

"With who?" Artemisa asked the lobby she now stood in alone.

Artemisa was more than happy to wait until Mr Magaldi had completed his business and was expecting a lengthy wait. What she was not expecting, however, was Tony coming back out. Artemisa did, however, notice he was walking differently. He was now more heavily armed; she noticed the weight shift.

She instinctively crouched to re-tie her shoelaces, subtly removed the knife from her boot and tucked it up her sleeve.

"Mr. Magaldi would like a word with you now," Tony said.

Artemisa nodded and followed him, unsure as to why he was now armed, and unsure what she expected to find once she entered Mr Magaldi's office.

What Artemisa found was Mr Magaldi sitting behind his desk, alone, waiting for her.

"Thank you, Tony," he said, as he dismissed the man.

As the door closed behind Artemisa, he said, "Take a seat, my dear, please."

Artemisa sat, her knife still in her sleeve, waiting for Mr Magaldi to speak. He let the silence simmer for a few minutes before he eventually said, "My dear, we are a day away from the most important moment in the history of this city. The consolidation of every piece of organised crime, under one roof. This roof. Through your guidance I am now in the safest building in the country, we can complete the final stages."

"I am happy for you," Artemisa began.

"I just need your assistance with one final matter," he interrupted. "This business meeting is with gang leaders and other business owners, such as myself."

Artemisa knew what was coming, he was going to ask her to murder them all, and she was not prepared to walk into a room and murder without being provoked.

"My dear, will you accompany me into the room, as opposed to Nicoletta, and watch them, with your military experience? If you think my life is in danger, press this button and Tony will arrive with back-up," Mr Magaldi said, handing her a mobile phone and indicating the button. "Keep me alive through this exchange," he implored.

'*At least I'm not being asked to kill them*', she thought as she left, reluctantly accepting the mobile.

Artemisa felt ill as she put on the suit and greeted Nicoletta and Tony the next evening. And after a long, few hours of standing in the corner, not saying anything, she got her instructions and followed Mr Magaldi into the room.

Sat around the polished oak table, that Artemisa was incredibly glad she had not had to carry, were twenty men, each with an associate standing behind them, backs against the wall.

Mr Magaldi took his seat at the head of the table and announced, "Gentleman, shall we begin?"

Before anyone could respond, he began what Artemisa could only assume was a very rehearsed speech, "Gentleman, we are at a crossroads. Every day the federal government and police officers of this great city pick us off faster than we can buy them off, and why? Because of the in-fighting of those sitting around this table. Rather than looking across this table and seeing a friend, a brother, a business partner, too many see an enemy, a rival. This mentality must end if we are to survive, and the plan I have to put before you all will guarantee survival."

He allowed for a short pause before saying, "Many of you may be thinking, why now? And the answer to that question is to show you I have nothing to hide. Because if we look deep within and ask ourselves the harsh questions we know, I could have waited 18 months and called this meeting and I would not have had to get my assistant here to lay out so many chairs, as there would only be a handful of people joining me around this table."

There was a harsh truth to this, Artemisa could tell as it was written across the faces of those who sat at the table.

"I agree, there is some need," one of the men eventually said. "But THIS, THIS is all of our empires becoming one, under you."

"This is survival," Mr Magaldi said simply. "If you had an

alternative, with all due respect, it would have been implemented by now."

Silence followed this, a silence nobody dared break. As it stretched, Artemisa's finger slid over the button on the phone ready to call Tony in for more back up, sensing that whoever did dare break this silence would do it with an outburst.

Finally, after what was an eternity, somebody furthest down the table said, "You can take everything, but I want no part of it. If this is the way it is going, then I am retiring. Better retired than working for you."

Artemisa watched as he signed the documents in front of him, before handing them to his assistant, who delivered it to Artemisa, who in turn set the documents down in front of Mr Magaldi. After placing the documents down, Artemisa watch the man and his assistant leave the room.

One by one they began to sign the documents, some opting to work for Mr Magaldi, some opting to retire.

Soon, there were about 13 people still seated around the table, their associates behind them.

"Well, gentleman?" he asked the remaining people. "What will it be? Will you scrounge around for scraps like dogs, or will you eat like royalty at the table?"

Silence.

"I would have almost respected you more if you took it all in a bloody coup," one of them eventually said.

There was a murmur of an agreement to this.

"It can be arranged. However, I would not want it to come to that," Mr Magaldi said, his fingertips pressed together underneath his chin.

Artemisa knew that this was the careless cigarette that would start the wildfire. The men all jumped to their feet at the mention of a coup. Artemisa began tapping the button on the phone as if there was no tomorrow, and if Mr Magaldi wasn't careful there might not be.

Mr Magaldi jumped to his feet, attempting to de-escalate the situation, but it was futile. Guns were being drawn. Artemisa's instincts took over before she could really think about whether or not this was a good idea.

She kicked Mr Magaldi behind his knees, so his weight gave way and he hit the floor, as she threw the knife towards the quickest to draw their gun.

Artemisa leapt onto the table and began throwing punches; she was clearly rusty. Everyone who tried to fight died, yet Artemisa did not end the fight without a few bruises, a cut above her eye and a bloody lip and cheek. She used whoever was in her reach as a shield, before launching them aside and throwing punches at every person not yet crumpled on the floor.

When everyone was dead, apart from her and Mr Magaldi, she rounded on him, a fury in her eye. However, when she saw the expression on Mr Magaldi's face, it halted the fury she was about to unleash on him. He had a euphoric look on his face, as if he had just watched something glorious.

She threw the phone down in front of Mr Magaldi before saying, "If that is the response time for Tony and the rest of your security, there is no help for you, unfortunately."

"My dear, I thank you."

"Consider it my leaving present," Artemisa panted, reaching for her glass, "That is why I came here yesterday. This isn't what I signed up for. I want out."

"Artemisa, think about it. What we have just achieved," he exclaimed, waving his hand at the dead bodies. "We are now on the cusp of greatness. We now OWN New York; this city is mine."

"You are on the cusp of greatness. I don't want greatness, I want quiet," she replied, the glint and look in her eye still very prominent.

She could see his shock, though. The mask was slipping, he thought she would accept his role as personal assistant, personal assassin.

"I understand we are on different paths, however, I will never forget what you have done for us here today. I will arrange for you a leaving gift, if you allow me one more favour."

"You want me and Tony to dump these bodies."

Mr Magaldi looked shocked that she knew this, not

knowing that Artemisa had seen Tony's shadow under the door. "We don't dump bodies, Artemisa, but yes." He gave her the address of an Italian restaurant.

"This will be my leaving gift for you," Artemisa offered.

She and Tony piled the bodies up and drove them through New York, and left the cars outside the Italian restaurant.

"Been a pleasure working with you, Tony," Artemisa said awkwardly, before heading in one direction leaving Tony standing there.

Once she was sure she could not be seen by Tony, Artemisa broke into a jog. She wanted to get back to the apartment, get her stuff and leave New York as soon as possible.

Artemisa stuffed her Gameboy, games, music player - all her worldly possessions, along with some clothes and as much cash as she could fit into the backpack, and headed towards the door.

Chapter Six:

Before Artemisa could reach the door handle, there was a knock.

Artemisa froze, her eyes darted towards the fire escape.

There was another knock at the door.

Artemisa darted towards the fire escape, her boots crunching on the snow as she darted down the stairs. As she ran, she heard the door burst open and guns start firing.

Artemisa sprinted as fast as she could without slipping on the snow and ice. She ran for four blocks before flagging down a taxi.

"Where to?"

"Train station, nearest one and there is a fifty-dollar tip if you get me there as soon as possible."

"You running from someone, young lady?" he asked, as he drove.

"Yeah, just go."

"Understood."

He didn't say a word for the rest of the journey, but delivered Artemisa quickly. She left him with 100 dollars before darting inside the train station, leaving blood droplets on his seats.

Artemisa didn't even register where she bought a ticket

to, but headed to the bathroom, disposing of her suit jacket and changing into jeans in a stall.

As Artemisa washed her face in the sink, she noticed the door open behind her. A woman in a sharp suit walked into the bathroom, not to a stall but to the bathroom mirror next to Artemisa.

Artemisa saw, in the reflection, a gun holstered to the woman's waist. Had Mr Magaldi alerted a Fed to her existence or was this a coincidence?

Artemisa didn't want to fight, so she saw her bruised face in the mirror and took a gamble. Using her teeth, she peeled a layer of skin from her lip so it made her eyes water, and she began to sob.

"Are you okay, hunny?" the woman asked her, looking at the bruises on her face.

"I am fine, I just need to make it on my train. I'm going to my mummy's," Artemisa whimpered.

"Are you escaping someone?" she asked, clearly startled by the bruises rapidly forming on Artemisa's jaw, cheekbone and eye socket.

Artemisa nodded, covering her face.

"My name is Sandi Lina, Federal Officer. I'll take you to your platform, we are here searching for someone dangerous."

Artemisa put up her hood to conceal her face and let

Sandi Lina escort her onto the train.

The train pulled away and Artemisa let out a sigh of relief. If Mr Magaldi had someone in the C.I.A. and had made them aware of her existence, she would need to keep on the move. American facial recognition would be looking for her now.

As panic rose, Artemisa steadied herself with the reassuring thought that if they did know she was alive, it would be a heavily compartmentalised secret, so only the C.I.A. would be after her. She needed to move fast, quiet and be strategic.

After three days, eight trains and five hours of sleep, Artemisa was not in good shape. She was exhausted, she was hungry, and she needed a shower.

Artemisa let out a sigh of relief when she looked around the shitty Midwest town she was in. She reckoned that she had at least five days before she was picked up by the surveillance state and the C.I.A.

Artemisa paid for her hotel room in cash, put the do not disturb sign on the door, and threw herself down on the bed. She was exhausted but could not get to sleep. The more she thought about Mr Magaldi betraying her to the C.I.A., the angrier she felt. Richard Cherry must have given him a C.I.A. contact. It was the only explanation as to why someone knocked on her door, and there were Feds at every train station within minutes of her quitting his employment. They may not have been given an up-to-date photo of her, but they were looking for her that night, whether they noticed or not.

Anger meant that when Artemisa awoke, she was not refreshed in the slightest. She walked across the quiet town and into the diner, thinking that she would plan her next move once she had a full stomach.

"I ain't seen you around here before," the person behind the counter said to Artemisa, as she placed her order.

"I'm just passing through," Artemisa muttered.

"Nobody really passes through these parts."

"I am nobody," Artemisa said, waiting patiently for her drink.

"You running from someone?" she asked, looking at Artemisa's face, where the bruises were still prominent.

"Nope, just waiting for my breakfast and drink before I move on."

"It's coming, it's coming," the woman said, clearly irritated by how unresponsive Artemisa was being.

As Artemisa waited for her food, she noticed the waitress texting someone, her eyes constantly darting over to where Artemisa was.

Artemisa devoured the sausages, bacon, and hash browns. As she slid out of her booth, she froze as a sheriff walked in, greeted the woman, removed his hat, and began making his way towards her.

"Greetings, can I have a moment of your time?"

"I am on a tight schedule," Artemisa muttered.

"It'll only take a moment," he said, blocking her path. "Are you running from someone?"

"Nope, travelling across the country to see family."

"Your bruises and cuts are causing some good people to be worried about you."

"I occasionally fight for money, these things happen," Artemisa lied coolly, doing her best to keep her temper under control.

"You planning on causing trouble around these parts?"

Artemisa exhaled through her nose and closed her eyes before saying through gritted teeth, "Not unless people keep standing in my way. I just need to rest and be on my way."

The sheriff let her past and Artemisa went back to the hotel room and slammed the door.

"What the fuck do I do now?" Artemisa asked her reflection in the mirror. She was hoping to have slept more and stayed another night; this seemed unlikely now.

Artemisa stood at the mirror as she contemplated her future. Although sticking to small towns meant it may take longer for the C.I.A. to find her, with less security cameras than a big city she stuck out like a sore thumb. However, with Christmas coming up, the amount of people in big cities meant she would not be noticed by anyone and crowds may hide her despite the increase in surveillance cameras.

Artemisa collected her bag, bought a map, and made her way to the train station.

"Where are we heading?" she was asked at the ticket office.

"What is the longest journey?"

"About six hours if you're heading west."

"Then take me west."

"Understood."

Artemisa sat in a quiet compartment and let the world blur past her in the window.

Artemisa was annoyed for allowing herself to be manipulated by Magaldi after escaping the U.S. government, but now she knew what to look out for, she knew the warning signs, all she needed to do was go off the grid, be forgotten about, go unseen and then she could focus on building a new life.

Six hours later, Artemisa departed the train and made her way through a city she was too tired to know the name of, until she found a hotel with vacancies.

'The Christmas period will make being on the run more difficult', Artemisa thought as she put the do not disturb sign on the door.

Artemisa craved sleep and thankfully it came to her soon; vivid dreams meant it was by no means peaceful sleep, but Artemisa woke up with a clearer perspective on her situation.

Artemisa spent the Christmas and New Year period in the hotel, going from her room to the hotel gym, hotel bar and restaurant, only occasionally leaving to go for a walk around the block, feeling the crunch of snow underfoot.

January was cold and miserable, and Artemisa was awoken most mornings by the sound of the wind howling. Artemisa knew the importance of being calm, collected and unseen but she was beginning to get bored after three weeks.

With the weather as foul as it was, Artemisa chanced a walk round the city, truly stretching her legs.

Artemisa allowed herself two hours of walking before returning to the hotel room, the fear of what would happen if she was caught by the C.I.A. crippling her into being reserved.

The next day, Artemisa again spent longer outside, taking in the city and getting fresh air into her lungs.

"Where have you been hiding, Artemisa?" a voice said quietly, as Artemisa waited at a crossing.

She froze, looking to the woman who stood to her right with a scarf wrapped around her face, and a hat, so only her glasses were visible.

"Ashton Potter, C.I.A. We've been looking for you for a few weeks, can I buy you a drink?"

"We insist," another voice said to her left.

Artemisa took her hands out of her pocket and clenched them into fists. "You've been looking for me, I should be flattered."

"Don't cause a scene and follow us," Ashton Potter said calmly.

"Got a family, Ashton?" Artemisa replied.

"What?" she asked, taken aback by the question.

"Cause if you do, chasing after me is going to upset your children when they are orphaned. So pretend you didn't see me and walk away."

"MOVE!" the man to her left ordered.

Artemisa didn't like his tone and knew she needed to act fast. "You've got me, let's go."

She took half a step before grabbing hold of the man's wrist, and like she did to Richard Cherry all those months ago, waited for him to die. With one dead she swung at Ashton Potter, who had already made a dart to see to her colleague and missed.

Artemisa saw more people exit cars all around and knew she was not going to be able to fight her way out of this situation, so she ran, tightening her backpack as she heard people begin to give chase.

Artemisa cut down side streets and overturned dustbins as she ran, trying to put as much distance between her and those chasing. As she stopped for breath, she noticed a lorry parked at a gas station. Sensing an opportunity to escape, she darted towards the lorry. She was about to climb inside when a voice shouted to her.

"Do not even think about hitching a ride in there."

Artemisa turned to the trucker and said, "Two hundred dollars."

"Deal!"

Artemisa clambered aboard and sat herself on top of a chest of drawers.

"How far do you wanna go, kid?" the trucker asked.

"How far are you going?"

"About 100 miles or so."

"Just drop me at a small town somewhere 50 miles away."

The ride was uncomfortable as fuck. She was shaking violently, but Artemisa had to reason that it got her out of town, and soon enough she was being told that this was her stop.

She thanked and paid the trucker before moving. It was late at night so she sat on a bench outside a bank and waited, the freezing air biting at her skin.

When the bank opened, she withdrew more cash, bought

a banged-up car that looked like it would get her a few miles, filled it with gas, and began to drive, knowing Ashton Potter was likely still following her.

The C.I.A. clearly thought they could capture and redeploy her as they saw fit, but she was done. She was nobody's puppet, nobody's pawn. She was Artemisa, SHE was death and they would regret fucking with her.

Artemisa drove, with the relief that local law enforcement would not get involved, so all she had to do was outthink Ashton Potter and she would be okay. After all, how hard could that be? After a while the lack of sleep began creeping up on her. Although she craved putting as many miles between her and those chasing her as possible, she knew it would be frivolous if she fell asleep in the driver's seat.

Artemisa found a roadside motel. She paid for the night, cut the security camera near her door, and went into the room. As Artemisa put her head down on the pillow, she found the motel was almost exclusively being used for people having extramarital affairs, based on the conversations and noises Artemisa could hear through the walls as she fell asleep.

Artemisa awoke suddenly, only a few hours later. Not because of the assorted sounds coming from next door- they seemed to have tired themselves out - but as she heard what sounded like multiple car doors slamming.

Artemisa chanced a look out of the window, there were

six cars that had pulled up, blacked-out windows and no license plates.

Artemisa scrambled for her clothes and backpack. As she did she noticed a small red light on her backpack, intermittently flashing.

Artemisa swore as she ripped the tracker off her bag, knowing it must have activated as soon as it connected to the motel Wi-Fi. She stamped it into the carpet before returning to the window.

They were surrounding the motel, spreading themselves thin. Artemisa only presumed Ashton Potter was speaking to the front desk, asking for a room key.

Ground floor, and close to her car, Artemisa knew she would be able to escape, but not without taking a few casualties. Artemisa slipped out of the room, locked the door, and crouched behind the ice machine, waiting.

Anticipation cut her breath short, Artemisa bit her tongue as she heard the voice of Ashton Potter directing her pawns.

Artemisa felt beads of sweat begin to run down her forehead, as Ashton Potter walked past the ice machine.

"As I open the door, everyone in, surround the room, I want to give her nowhere to go. Nobody makes a sound until she is surrounded," Ashton ordered.

Artemisa watched the key go in the door, and everyone entered before she acted. She locked the door behind them, left the key in the door in a hope of somewhat trapping them and made a dart towards the car.

Six people were left in the car park as the rest secured the perimeter. Artemisa ran at them, throwing punches as she made her way to her car.

Blessing the hybrid making no noise, she reversed and sped out of the car park. Leaving the six dead bodies around an empty car parking space, Artemisa drove the speed limit; not wanting to be pulled over, but knowing they would be hot on her heels.

Artemisa took right and left turns with no idea where the road would lead, until she found herself on a freeway.

Her hands shook violently on the steering wheel as she drove, her eyes stinging and a self-hatred for getting herself in this situation festering in the pit of her stomach.

Caffeine pumped through her veins and the frosty morning sun shone as Artemisa filled the tank before continuing on her drive. She did not know what state she was in, where the nearest city was or how far behind her the tenacious Ashton Potter would be.

After seven bodies, Artemisa hoped someone would see the sense in letting her vanish into thin air, as opposed to throwing people in her way, but she was doubtful and was not going to take the risk.

Artemisa pulled off the freeway hours later and found herself in a town, and to her relief, there was a train station. She booked a ticket to head deep into Kentucky.

She needed a shower and sleep more than anything in life; stress, fear, and exhaustion were causing her to see things. She fidgeted more than she ever had, and with no food lining her stomach, the sickness she felt was excruciating.

Artemisa held the door open to an elderly gentleman with a walking stick on the train as he attempted to get off. However as his hand brushed her she flinched back, knowing she almost killed him, despite not wanting to.

As Artemisa stepped off the train, she vomited into a bin on her way out, which made people give her a wide berth. The city she was in had a couple of different hotels; the first had no vacancies, the second thankfully did.

The man on the front desk looked genuinely concerned as he handed Artemisa a key and escorted her to her hotel room. He said it was for common courtesy, but as Artemisa caught a look at herself in the mirror, it was to ensure she didn't pass out in the elevator. She looked like fucking shit.

Artemisa sat in the shower, not confident in her ability to not pass out if she stood, before crawling across to the bed and under the covers.

Nineteen hours later, the lack of food of the past few days awoke her, and she changed before heading out to get something to eat.

She bought new clothes from a shop on the way back to the hotel room; the clothes she was wearing were no longer clean, but after returning to the room she got back into bed, knowing she would need to move on sooner rather than later.

The car Artemisa had used was still at the train station car park, so it wouldn't be too difficult to check surveillance cameras in the cities along the different train routes.

It was fear that awoke Artemisa a few hours later. She checked the bedside clock and to her dismay, it was four o'clock in the morning. She rolled to the floor and did a primitive workout until she presumed commuters would be heading to work and she would be able to blend in with a crowd on her way to public transport.

The crippling sensation in the pit of Artemisa's stomach never shifted, the anxiety worsened, and her neck muscles hurt as she constantly looked over her shoulder.

Artemisa bought a pair of fake glasses with thick frames, in a bid to slow down facial recognition from security cameras. She also bought a bigger backpack, able to hold more clothes and still be lightweight enough for her to carry. She repacked her bag, depositing the old one in a bin before moving on.

She was lamenting her situation and was sick to death of watching the world pass her by from the window of a train. More than the boredom and self-hatred she felt about being in this situation, Artemisa felt her sense of reality begin to slip; the lack of sleep and a proper meal, and the freedom of not needing to look over her shoulder.

Artemisa checked into her motel and made her way across to a bar and grill, desperate for food and a drink.

She sat in the corner, trying not to draw attention to herself. Unfortunately for Artemisa, being alone and being a woman was seemingly enough attention, as she noticed a group looking at her from the other side of the bar as she polished off her burger.

Artemisa's fingers shook, her cutlery scraping the plate as she noticed the group still staring at her. As Artemisa avoided eye contact with them she knew a universal truth, if any of them touched her, they would die. She didn't know if she would be able to control it.

"Can I get you anything else?" the bartender asked, as she collected Artemisa's plate, causing her to jump.

"If you can get that group over there to stop staring at me and pretend I didn't exist then I'll add twenty dollars to your tip," Artemisa said, trying to be casual, but her clenched, shaking fists gave her away.

"Sure, they don't dare cause trouble when I am on shift, but I'll give 'em a little reminder."

"Thank you."

Credit where credit was due, Artemisa was left well alone and she was able to finish her drink in peace. She left the bartender a tip as she promised and left the bar.

Artemisa was followed from the bar. It was expected, but Artemisa was not in the mood for it. She stopped in the car park and turned; they stopped as well.

Artemisa waited for one of them to say something or move, but they just stopped, unsure how to proceed.

Artemisa did not unclench her fists but walked on. Not in the mood to commit murder, she stretched her legs, walking a few miles before returning to the hotel room.

If they followed her, then they had signed their own death warrant, but Artemisa was not looking to leave a breadcrumb trail of bodies for the C.I.A. to find, especially as they were already actively searching for her.

Artemisa couldn't sleep. These small towns with one motel meant if people were looking for her then it was easy to know where she would be. The fear paralysed her and tightened the knot in her stomach, so she sat, unable to occupy her mind, unable to sleep and allow herself to recharge.

As Artemisa made her way to the train station to move on, she decided a bigger city was needed, as opposed to a one motel town.

'You look like shit', she thought, when she caught her reflection in the window. The lack of sleep and the constant tension was causing her to crack.

She flinched as someone brushed past her, terrified of

accidentally killing someone. She couldn't understand why she was losing control, even when she was under lock and key on a military base she was always in control, but now, now she was slipping. Artemisa needed to regain control before innocent people began getting hurt.

As the train trundled along, Artemisa realised there would be no help books, websites or people that she could seek advice from on exactly HOW to regain control; this would be a journey of self-discovery Artemisa was unsure she was ready for.

Her fear got worse as the train trundled on, an elderly lady bumped into her on the way back from the train toilets and as their skin touched, Artemisa worried she had killed the poor woman.

Once she departed the train, Artemisa found a hotel and barricaded herself in her room. She sat, legs crossed on the bed, and took a deep breath. She needed to stop being chased. After two hours, this was the conclusion she had come to, she would be dead soon if she kept this up.

The question Artemisa kept asking herself was how many people would the C.I.A. throw at her before they gave up, giving the illegality of the bulk of her life and the blood on her hands?

Artemisa didn't really want to just murder all of the people who were after her, but she was beginning to think that this would be her only option.

She ordered room service so that she would not need to leave the room or see anyone, and sank into the hotel bath before it arrived. She felt slightly better once she had eaten, relaxed in the bath and curled up under the covers. She fell into an uneasy sleep.

Artemisa awoke and ordered breakfast to her room. She didn't want to leave her hotel room but with no access to the internet, she needed to leave.

She slunk down to the business suite and sat in the corner, vaguely researching self-control and methods to keep herself centred, but none of it proved very helpful and she slunk back towards her room.

Chapter Seven:

After three days, Artemisa was getting restless, having not left the hotel since she arrived, but knowing that leaving the hotel increased the likelihood of her being spotted if they were indeed on her tail.

Artemisa enjoyed going from shop to shop and forced herself to buy a book, something to concentrate on. She also bought some jewellery to aid her aesthetic; thick rings sat on each of her fingers, not only giving her something to fidget with, but now if she were to get into a fistfight, the rings would be connecting with an opponent before the rest of her fist, meaning that if she wanted them alive, they would remain that way; in theory at least.

Artemisa walked in circles to see if she was being followed, but she noticed nobody walking a similar pattern to her or any cars that followed her. She was in the clear, so returned to the hotel.

As Artemisa walked through the lobby, she noticed the bar was busier than normal, but paid it no heed as she walked past the reception. She noticed someone that looked suspiciously like Ashton Potter with a few associates checking into the hotel.

Artemisa stopped to tie her shoelace, hidden from view as she heard one of them say, "We know she is in the city somewhere; we'll rest tonight and begin the search tomorrow. Ben Austin, I want you running all traffic cameras from crack of dawn tomorrow, and get Peter Matthews to have agents at every bus port, train station and private airport, go to your rooms and get some rest."

Once Artemisa heard the hotel rooms they were staying in, she sprinted up the stairs as fast as she could and into her own room. Artemisa couldn't catch her breath. She shook violently as she put everything in her backpack.

She knew she needed to kill them all and slip out of the city, but that was easier said than done. They were in three hotel rooms on the floor below her.

Artemisa splashed water on her face and looked at her reflection. She was not in control of her power, so she knew she needed to be swift, precise and quiet if she ever wanted to experience the blissful peace of safety again.

Artemisa sank onto the floor, her back to the door and waited, her arms wrapped around her knees. She didn't know what she needed to gain control, but the anxiety in her stomach constricted like a knot and Artemisa could not untie it.

When the clock in her room struck two o'clock, she removed the rings from her knuckles and left her hotel room. She crept down the deserted hallways until she arrived outside the first hotel room.

Hotel doors were always embarrassingly easy to unlock. By the age of seven, she had picked a hotel room door and killed someone on behalf of the C.I.A., so this was child's play.

She slipped in, leaving the door ajar. Three men slept, no sign of Ashton Potter, but it wouldn't matter, those three men wouldn't be chasing her again.

She slipped into the second room, still no sign of Ashton Potter.

Artemisa's hands trembled to the extent that she struggled to open the door to the third hotel room; eventually she made her way inside, none of the people inside were Ashton Potter and Artemisa retched violently as she left the hotel room. Stress was becoming a real issue and it was affecting the mission as well as her health.

She had heard her, clear as day, say the hotel room numbers, there was no mistake and yet Artemisa couldn't complete the job, and if the job wasn't completed then Artemisa wasn't safe.

Artemisa made her way downstairs. Fighting the almost overwhelming urge to scream, she left the hotel and surveyed the darkness.

Artemisa began walking down the street, no direction planned. As she walked, she saw an all-night bodega. Before Artemisa could even open the door, she saw Ashton Potter, at the counter.

"Fuck's sake," Artemisa muttered to the night sky, before darting into the shadows.

Ashton Potter stepped into the night sky and said to herself, "This mission will be the fucking end of me," as she put a cigarette in between her teeth and fumbled with a lighter, her other hand clasped tightly on the bottle in her other hand.

"I did warn you of that," Artemisa said, stepping out of the shadows behind her.

Ashton spun around and leapt off the pavement onto the road in fright.

Artemisa sighed deeply before saying, "Your men in the hotel are dead, is this really worth it? Chasing me, getting people killed?"

"I'm just following orders," Ashton said, slipping her lighter back into her pocket.

"You're leading the lambs to slaughter. I'm tired of killing them and you sure as shit seem tired of chasing me. So ask yourself, what are you gonna do?"

"No. I'm tired of this cat and mouse bullshit. You're gonna come in quietly. This is the C.I.A. that you are dealing with and you're too valuable to defect, so make it easy on yourself."

"Listen here, you dumb fucking bitch," Artemisa howled, shaking more violently than ever before, "I am not defecting, I am not a puppet, I am done, so if I need to leave your broken body behind me then so be it," Artemisa said, walking backward, away from the bodega, into the darkness of the alleyway, knowing Ashton Potter was going to follow.

Predictably, Ashton Potter followed, the bottle in her hand now clenched as a weapon.

"And so we witness the last moments of Ashton Potter," Artemisa said.

Ashton didn't say anything, replying only with a punch towards Artemisa's midsection. Ashton clearly trained as a boxer, as she darted forward, swinging the bottle towards Artemisa's head.

The vodka smashed against the wall as shards of glass landed in Artemisa's hair and cut her cheek.

Artemisa let out a steadying sigh, as her fist connected with Ashton's ribs. Artemisa then threw Ashton over her shoulder, and she bounced off the concrete.

"I tried to warn you. May your death bring sense," Artemisa said solemnly, before delivering the final, devastating blow.

Artemisa walked away, shaking her head. If Ashton's words were true and they were scared of her working for another government, then they would keep hunting her until she was dead.

Artemisa headed towards the train station, knowing there may not be another train for a couple of hours. She sat on the platform and waited.

When the five o'clock train arrived, Artemisa took a window seat and fought back tears.

As the world passed her by, Artemisa couldn't hold back any longer, and the tears began to run down her cheeks, thick and fast. Artemisa didn't have the strength to wipe them away.

"Are you okay there, dear?" a voice said from the aisle.

Artemisa took her head off the window and looked round to see an old woman giving her a wide smile, but concern in her eyes.

"I, I am fine, thank you," Artemisa croaked, clearing her throat.

"Where are you heading, dear?"

"The, erm, final stop," Artemisa whispered, now wiping her eyes on her sleeve.

"Sometimes talking about things can help, would you mind if I sat down?"

"I just need to collect my thoughts. Thank you for the offer," Artemisa said, her voice a little firmer now, her eyes no longer watering.

"Okay, deary."

Artemisa appreciated the gesture. As she returned to looking out of the window, Artemisa realised that she needed to get all of the emotion out of her system, and then she would be able to re-focus on a plan.

When the train pulled into the station, Artemisa fastened her backpack and made her way towards the door. As she did, the old woman from earlier stood there with what she presumed was her grandson. Upon seeing Artemisa, she said, "If you ever need to talk, there is a church about six blocks away."

Artemisa laughed and said, "Not even God can help me, but thank you."

"Confession is completely anonymous. Stay safe, dear."

'*If there is a God, I must be the devil*', Artemisa thought as she walked. But on consideration, Artemisa thought maybe some advice on regaining control might help, and she didn't really have many other options, but on the way she saw a library, which Artemisa presumed could help her more than God could.

The self-help books were cringe-inducing, and although Artemisa felt sick, she didn't want to be ejected from the library for the mess.

Eventually, Artemisa found a book on Buddhism and meditation which seemed promising, but just before Artemisa could sink her teeth into the books, she was told that the library was having to close early.

As Artemisa left, she kept her head down and began walking, a plan formulating in her head as she walked back towards the train station.

"Where are you heading?" the ticket master asked her.

"A city with an international airport," Artemisa muttered.

Three trains later, Artemisa arrived and booked herself a flight for three days' time, and she made her way to a hotel, hoping and praying that by the time Ashton Potter's replacement had picked up her trail, it would be too late.

Artemisa only left the hotel room to get food and drinks from a local shop before returning to her room.

On the day of her flight, she was packing her bag when there was a knock on the door. "Room Service."

"Wrong room," Artemisa called out, dropping her bag by the door, and checking the door's peephole.

"Room 319?" the voice said again.

"No, thank you," Artemisa growled, as she searched the room for her t-shirt.

Artemisa heard the door unlock and she let out a sigh. Why did they always insist on trying to fight her?

Chapter Eight:

Artemisa spat blood onto the floor as she looked at the bodies piled onto the hotel carpet. She let out a deep sigh. These men didn't have to die. They could have been at home enjoying the sunshine, and yet here they were dead in a hotel room because they decided to come after her. And all she wanted was to be left alone.

Artemisa stepped over a crooked and broken leg to take the pen and napkin, both emblazoned with the hotel logo, and she wrote a very simple note: *'LEAVE ME ALONE'*. She placed the napkin on the bald head of the man on the top of the pile and hoped that they would finally take heed of her warnings, after all, how many disposable people did they have?

She walked over to the mirror and looked at her reflection. One of the bastards, now dead on the floor behind her, had managed to split her lip open with a well-connected punch, her lip had been opened so many times, if this healed it would definitely scar. But it didn't matter in comparison, the man who did it had still met his demise before he had met his demise. Since being on the run, Artemisa avoided looking at her reflection as all it showed was stress, exhaustion, and anxiety.

"That will make airport security so much easier," she said sarcastically to her reflection; a bruise on her eye socket and a cut or three around her jaw, this coupled with a few of her other bruises and cuts meant she looked like shit.

Five-foot-six, her hair swept over to the side right and the left side of her head shaved was a pleasant change to her normal long ponytail, and despite the hotel valet commenting on the "lesbian haircut", she preferred her hair this way and the pink and white was better than her normal natural red hair. Two days of sleep had done her well and now she was laser-focused, she looked better than she had in a long while.

She spent a bit of time admiring the intricate detail of her two sleeve tattoos, looking at where, if she ever found a moment to rest, she should get some filler. It felt like a lifetime ago she got the work done. She didn't regret leaving the mafia, but it had made her life a lot more stressful.

After some time looking at herself in the mirror she sighed, and decided it was time to get going. She put on her scuffed yet ever-reliable combat boots, jeans, a simple black shirt and zip-up hoodie. She travelled light, she didn't have a choice anymore.

Stepping over the bodies once more, she walked to the bedside table and began putting on her rings; thick, metallic and stylish, she could not go anywhere without them on. Ever since purchasing them they had become a bit of a lifeline, a constant thing to tinker with, keep her wrecked nerves somewhat in check.

One of the men had car keys in their pocket, and given the fact they were dead, they wouldn't have much need for a car.

Artemisa drew the curtains, put on her jacket, took one last swig of the bottle from the minibar, hitched her backpack over one shoulder, and left the room.

She took the stairs to the car park as opposed to the elevator, hoping to avoid the valet who escorted her up to her room. She was now borrowing a car from one of the bodies upstairs. She walked through the car park, clicking the key fob till she finally saw a response from a black sedan.

She adjusted the seat, put on her seatbelt, turned on the radio, and began to drive. The airport was 15 minutes away, Artemisa knew that once she was through security then she would be on the home stretch and hopefully safe and free.

Her heart was racing and Artemisa felt queasy; not a new feeling but a feeling that was still irritating. She parked the car, left the old mobile phone in the cup holder and walked towards the airport terminal.

As she walked, Artemisa checked the passport and had to remind herself that she had to pretend that 'Heidi Roberts' was not a new name to her. She could refer to herself as Artemisa again—once she landed. Artemisa began queuing at check-in; she began playing with the rings on her fingers, twisting them round absentmindedly.

She made it through check-in and finally passed airport security without any incidents. Past security, Artemisa bought some books to keep her entertained, put her MP3 player on and began listening to music, watching the people hustle and bustle their way through the airport.

Finally, her flight was called and Artemisa joined the people boarding the plane; she wouldn't stop feeling sick until they were airborne and the sickness and anxiety in her stomach was close to making her double over.

She boarded the plane after a lengthy queue and slumped into the aisle seat. The arrival of the men had interrupted her peaceful morning, packing what few belongings she owned. She thought the murder of Ashton Potter would have given her some breathing room for this trip. Now, however, Artemisa knew the C.I.A. would be following her, although she had a lengthy head start and a fake name which should slow them down, ever so slightly.

The plane began to fill and Artemisa began to fiddle with the rings on her fingers again. If she had been tracked through airport security, then she would be trapped on a plane full of innocent passengers.

Within half an hour the plane was in the air, and Artemisa let out a sigh of relief. If the U.S. government were going to come for her again they would have done it before take-off, not whilst airborne and no longer on U.S. soil.

She signalled the air hostess and requested a few drinks; if this didn't calm her nerves then nothing would.

Artemisa reached into her pocket, and with the drinks on the table began reading the breathing techniques she hastily scribbled down in the library. These breathing exercises and cheap cider might be the only thing that could keep her alive on this flight and she focused on them with all her might.

Artemisa really despised the fact that she couldn't sleep on aeroplanes. That she had never been able to was made worse because she didn't know when she would next be able to sleep, all she knew was she needed to get everything under control before someone got seriously hurt.

After a while, she picked up one of the fantasy books she had purchased in the terminal and began to read.

The book was finished before the plane landed, and as she was leaving the plane she surveyed everyone, making sure nobody was looking at her suspiciously.

It took two hours to get through airport security and eventually Artemisa stepped out of Osaka Kansai airport. Now she was here, Artemisa realised how little she had actually planned and how little of her plan she had thought through.

She went back inside and quickly bought a tourist guidebook to help her translate. She stopped a gentleman in a suit who looked like they weren't in a hurry, pointed to a picture of the train station, said "Kyoto" and tried to formulate a sentence with the guidebook.

He stopped her and to Artemisa's relief gave her instructions in English.

It was an hour-long train journey to Kyoto. Artemisa could feel tiredness starting to set in. Her eyelids were heavy and in order to stay awake, Artemisa decided pain would help so she bit down on her busted bottom lip.

As light as her backpack was, it was starting to feel heavy on her shoulders. She eventually took her seat on a bus heading out of the city.

Artemisa was forcing herself to stay awake as the bus trundled along a winding road. Hours later, Artemisa put music on to help her stay awake.

When the bus reached its final stop, the driver pointed her in the direction and told her it would be a long walk to the village. She thanked him and began walking towards what she hoped would be a turning point in her life.

She walked through the night and into the early morning sun. As the sun rose, she saw what she was looking for, down the hill was a small village and in the distance was a Buddhist temple.

Her belly growled for food and water, she bit her lip again and walked faster than she normally would. She didn't know what would happen when she reached the temple, but she was worried she would be turned away.

As she approached the temple, she noticed monks stop to look at her. She bowed to each of them in turn and stopped at the bottom of the steps. The sickness was back but she was unsure whether or not this was due to a lack of sleep, food, water, or nerves.

"Why are you here, Gaijin?" a monk asked her.

"I have come to learn the art of meditation, learn the Buddhist way of meditation," Artemisa said, her hands in front of her, the rings on her fingers being span around as her fingers shook.

After a few minutes of silence, where Artemisa felt close to throwing up, a monk finally spoke to her, "I am Monk Ryo, follow me."

She quickened her pace and followed the monk. They walked for five minutes. He sat under a tree and invited Artemisa to do the same. She crossed her legs and waited for him to speak, stomach clenched.

"Why have you travelled here? Why have you travelled so far? With no sleep, no food or water?" Monk Ryo said after a few minutes.

"I need to learn to meditate, centre myself, find balance and peace safely," Artemisa said, her heart racing. "I have travelled a long way, that is true, by plane, by bus and by foot, but it will be worth it."

"To learn this, you have travelled all the way here? Not

from a book in the west?"

"That would be a pale imitation, I cannot afford to settle for a pale imitation," Artemisa said, clicking two of her rings together.

"Wait here," he said, after what felt like an eternity.

Artemisa watched as she watched Monk Ryo walk back towards the temple. When he eventually returned with two cups and a pot of tea, he settled himself, handed a cup to Artemisa, and poured out the steaming brew into the cup she clutched in grateful hands.

"Tell me your earliest memory," he eventually requested.

"It isn't a happy one," Artemisa said, taking a sip of tea, "aged three, sat in a straitjacket watching cartoons on a television. All the while doctors run tests on me." She twitched. She did not like thinking about the early parts of her life, when they tried to figure out how she killed people before turning her skills to better use.

"What is so important about centring yourself? Why do you believe meditation is key to all this?"

"I... I used to be able to control everything, I mastered it. Now, not so much. I am a danger to myself and to everyone else if I do not learn what I have travelled here to learn," Artemisa stammered, after taking a sip of the tea. She didn't want to reveal what she could do but felt like it would be inevitable soon enough.

He watched her drink her tea with piercing eyes. "People will get hurt if you do not master control?"

Artemisa nodded.

Monk Ryo watched her drink the rest of the cup before he instructed her to follow him towards the temple. Once inside, Monk Ryo picked up a small wooden box. He turned to her opening it saying, "Your rings, Gaijin, as well as your other belongings."

Artemisa growled as she took her rings off her fingers and placed them in the box. They were a coping mechanism as much as an aesthetic. She placed her music player and Gameboy in the box as well. All of her coping mechanisms were locked away.

"You play with them when you're nervous."

Another monk approached and led her back outside.

"Sit," he instructed, "close your eyes."

Artemisa followed his commands and sat, legs crossed and her hands in her lap, trembling ever so slightly.

"Back straight, not too rigid, not too relaxed."

Artemisa could feel sickness start to rise in her stomach again. Her back was not against a wall, and she could sense people in her blind spots.

"Ignore the fact you don't know what is around you," he

snapped.

Artemisa tried to put these thoughts to the back of her mind and convinced herself that she was safe here in a distant Buddhist temple in Kyoto. If they ever found her, it would be weeks from now, she was safe.

"Breath from the abdomen," she heard the monk say. "One breath at a time, deep breaths in, deep breaths out."

The monk became silent, letting Artemisa breath.

"Acknowledge all thoughts that come into your mind, do not engage with them, let them pass," he said after a short while.

Artemisa wondered what she was meant to do when this happened and endeavoured to not engage with these thoughts. However, she thought that acknowledging them and not engaging with them was counterintuitive.

She did not know how long she sat there, nor what was happening in the background, but a noise behind her made her go from a sitting position into a fighting stance within a second, her eyes open, fists clenched. She was breathing deeply.

She was looking at Monk Ryo and the other monk looked back at her with a blank expression, she did not sense the other monk move.

"Gaijin, Monk Shoda did not tell you to stop meditating.

You must be mindful of your surroundings but not react to them."

Artemisa slowly sat back down, her eyes stinging from the light. She crossed her legs, readjusting her hands and tried to compose herself once again. She was painfully aware they were watching her; it went against every aspect of her training allowing the strangers to be in her blind spots once again.

She did not know how long she had been sitting there but Artemisa began to fidget; tiredness, hunger, restlessness, and anxiety all starting to creep in and affect her body and mind.

"That is enough, Gaijin," Monk Shoda said, after watching her fidget and move for a few minutes.

Artemisa uncurled her legs and stretched, her stomach grumbling as she did.

"Thoughts?" Monk Ryo asked her.

"I don't know how to not focus on thoughts, let them go when they come into my mind," she said honestly.

"Come and eat, you look hungry," Monk Ryo said, pointing the way for Artemisa to go.

Artemisa was sitting away from everyone else. She normally kept her distance, so she didn't accidentally kill someone, and she was grateful for the space. In this instant, however, it was the monks who kept their distance from her. It didn't faze her, but she was curious as to why it was only Monk Ryo and Monk Shoda who spoke to her.

After she had eaten her fill, Monk Ryo took Artemisa to a secluded corner of the temple and gave her a roll mat to sleep on. Artemisa curled up on the floor with her back against the wall and was ready to sleep until sunrise.

Sunrise came far too early for Artemisa's liking. She washed and changed into clothes given to her by Monk Ryo and she followed the small monk as he led her towards the sunrise.

They sat, eyes closed, facing the rising sun. The breeze was nice on her face, and Artemisa allowed herself a smile. It was the first day in a long time where she truly felt calm; Artemisa truly felt like she could rest here.

"Do you hear that bird?" Monk Ryo asked her, after a while of silence.

Artemisa did not answer immediately, instead choosing to listen to the sounds of nature all around her, before she eventually said, "I do."

"Can you make that bird stop? Can you change the noise the bird makes?"

"No."

"Then it is of no concern to you. Acknowledge the bird noise, listen to it but do not spend any energy on it, give it no attention, pay it no heed. Simply acknowledge and then move on."

Artemisa nodded as Monk Ryo went silent. She readjusted her position and took a deep inhale. It was a strange sensation, the cat and mouse aspect of her life recently had not left her with time to sit and breathe.

A short while later, she sensed Monk Ryo stand and leave but Artemisa stayed put. She stayed until she heard the crunch of footsteps on grass behind her and Monk Shoda say, "Come."

Artemisa opened her eyes into the dazzling sun, stood and followed the monk. He led her to what he called a zen garden. It was rather beautiful, Artemisa conceded, looking at the rocks and the gravel. She was unsure what her purpose was around this beautiful representation of nature.

Monk Shoda handed her a rake and pointed to the gravel. Artemisa understood what he wanted her to do. She breathed, counting the breaths she took in and out, and began to rake the gravel from one end to the other. She took it slow and felt a wave of relief as she did this.

She did not know and did not care how long she did this for, and only realised how thirsty she was when Monk Ryo and Monk Shoda came over with tea.

Artemisa let out a deep breath from her diaphragm before she sat, and gratefully accepted the cup of tea. She let the steam rise into her face before she took a sip.

"You are shaking less," Monk Ryo said, looking at Artemisa's hands.

"I had not noticed," Artemisa confessed.

"You seemed at peace working on the Kare Sansui."

"It was calming," Artemisa said, after finishing her cup of tea. "I found it helpful."

Monk Ryo's expression was unreadable as he instructed her to follow. Artemisa thought that he would be an excellent poker player but doubted whether or not he would partake in such activities.

He instructed her to breathe once they were both seated. She could feel his eyes on her and it made her uncomfortable, but she resigned herself to the fact that she could not change it, and therefore it was not worth her attention.

Soon, however, Artemisa sensed that it was not just her and Monk Ryo who were sat together, other monks were sitting around her, meditating just like her.

Artemisa tried to tell herself that she could not change this, so it was not worth her attention. But her breathing was no longer deep and slow but quick and shallow. She felt her knuckles clench and she was soon thinking about the escape routes from the room she was currently in.

After a while she conceded and opened her eyes, arose and walked out. Looking at her fingers, they were trembling. Artemisa knew she would be scolded for leaving the meditation session without permission, but she sank down against the wall, wrapped her arms around her legs, and let out short, trembling breaths. retching as she fought back the impulse to throw up.

"How can you handle cities and the commotion of the west if you cannot handle monks meditating?" Monk Ryo asked from above her.

"I didn't," Artemisa replied, "or I had vices."

"You have neither here," he stated, a fact that was painfully obvious to Artemisa. "You are here to learn, and part of learning is failure. Come walk with me."

Artemisa stood up and followed the monk. As they walked he did not say a word, only instructing Artemisa continue at the same pace as him. This pained her, as his pace was slower than hers, but she followed his instructions. His lack of speed was infuriating, but she did not break step.

After seven or so laps, Monk Ryo led her back to the group and she returned to her original sitting position.

Artemisa struggled through this session but she did not leave again, and when the other monks departed, she let out a sigh of relief.

She stayed sat down, waiting for instruction from either

Monk Ryo or Monk Shoda, but none came. She closed her eyes and began to breathe, reminding herself that this is all part of the process she had come here to do.

Artemisa found herself in a routine over the next two weeks, and it suited her. She still struggled in group meditation sessions, but none were as bad as the day when she was forced to leave. Monk Ryo was always quick to comment on Artemisa's progress, and she could gradually feel the knot in her stomach untighten after each meditation.

On her 17th day at the temple, Monk Ryo called her into the secluded corner where she slept.

"You will be tested. Sit and meditate," he instructed.

Artemisa obliged and waited for this test.

She heard the test coming. It sounded like a gaggle of excitable children, and when she opened one eye to peer around the corner, it was exactly as she feared - a group of school children, Artemisa surmised, from the village she had seen when she walked to the temple.

They could not see her, which she was pleased about, and once she knew what the test was, then she could focus on her breathing. She reminded herself that she could not change the situation, and therefore it was of no concern to her.

Artemisa felt her breathing get quicker, and she ensured

it slowed back down, as she listened to the children from the village. She couldn't understand them, but the noise and volume of people was the challenge. It was difficult, and she could feel the anxiousness start to rise in her stomach again, but she did her best to pay it no attention.

They were clearly being given a lesson of some sorts, but Artemisa focused on what she had been told to do.

"How did you cope?" Monk Shoda asked her much later.

"Better than I thought I would," Artemisa replied, opening her eyes.

She watched as the children filed out of the temple, their lesson clearly over. Two adults approached Monk Ryo, and they talked in hushed voices, which made the hairs on the back of Artemisa's neck stand on end, even though they could not see her and she could not understand what was being said.

When the two men left, Monk Ryo sat back down, clearly deep in thought. After 20 minutes he stood and instructed Artemisa to follow him.

He walked to where they had first sat the day she arrived at the temple and handed her a cup of tea, placing between them a large bowl of water.

"I have another lesson for you."

Artemisa nodded, both hands clasped around the cup of tea.

"Look at the water in the bowl, it is still, tranquil."

"It is," Artemisa agreed, looking at the bowl through the steam of the teacup.

"Watch what happens when I drop a stone into it," he continued, dropping a small piece of gravel into the bowl.

"The water is no longer still, it ripples. The tranquillity is broken, and then it returns to the natural state," Artemisa observed.

"Yes, exactly," Monk Ryo agreed, dropping another stone in the bowl. "If I keep dropping stones into the water, it can never be tranquil, the water will always ripple."

"I am the water?" Artemisa questioned, sensing where this analogy was going.

"Police have been to the village, asking about a Gaijin with a silly haircut in different colours. They say they were sent by Americans in Kyoto, who are now working with local police."

Artemisa let out a groan. "I understand, I hoped I would be able to find peace here."

"You may still be able to find peace here, Gaijin, but you cannot be still like the water when there are stones being dropped into the water."

"Thank you for your teachings, Monk Ryo," Artemisa bowed deeply to the monk.

Artemisa changed from the robes provided to her by Monk Ryo and into the clothes she arrived in. She collected her possessions from the box and left the temple.

At the temple steps, she bowed once again to Monk Ryo and Monk Shoda, who bowed in turn.

Monk Ryo bowed before saying, "Travel safely, Gaijin."

Chapter Nine:

Artemisa turned and began the long walk to the bus stop where she had gotten off. As she walked, Artemisa began to plan a strategy of how she would leave Japan. Between Kyoto and Osaka, she would need a new passport, new clothes, and some form of deceptive clothing.

When she finally arrived back in Kyoto, she bought a new t-shirt, jacket, a hat, and a pair of glasses, and put on a face mask. As she walked around Kyoto, she kept her eye out for any tourists who looked like they would have their passport easy for the picking.

She had an hour's wait at the train station, after having no luck finding an American or European with a passport to 'borrow'. The only ones she saw were those who were protective of their belongings. She did not know if her Heidi passport was flagged, but she did not want to take the chance of being detained by police at the airport.

As the train approached the station, Artemisa noticed that there was a group of tourists also getting on the train. They spoke English, and Artemisa knew this would be the best chance of getting a passport.

She entered the carriage behind them, cautious not to draw attention to herself. She sat down next to the window as the train pulled out of the station. As the train picked up speed, she noticed the unmistakable signs of American C.I.A. agents on the platform. She sank down into her seat, hoping that she had not been spotted. With what was visible of her face, there was no guarantee she had been made, but she wanted to ensure that was the case.

Artemisa began looking up and down the train carriage. If there were Americans on the train platform, then there was a good chance there were Americans on the train as well.

She began to look around, all the while being very conscious that a blonde woman's purse looked to contain a passport.

Her timing would have to be impeccable, if she was to pull this off without any suspicion or being caught. Artemisa looked back out of the window and saw to her delight there was a tunnel approaching. This would be the opening she needed.

She shifted in her seat, making sure she was poised. As soon as the train entered the tunnel, Artemisa darted and with two fingers managed to pull the passport out of the purse with relative ease.

When the train exited the tunnel, Artemisa made her way to a different compartment of the train.

When she sat back down, she took deep, steadying breaths. Every indication was that she made the heist without arousing suspicion. She checked over the passport, memorising every detail should she be asked by airport security.

Once she was off the train, Artemisa began putting the next stages of her plan into action. The C.I.A. had taught her many great skills, which they were now presumably regretting doing, and she would use each and every one of them to her advantage. She found a secluded workplace and got to work, making the necessary amendments to the passport to get her back into the U.S.A. undetected.

She had not spent as long as she would have liked learning from the monks, but it had served her purpose to an extent. She could now brush someone's skin with her own and they would not collapse, slip into a coma or die.

However, it was becoming clear to Artemisa that she would need to get the shovel out and dig a few more graves, if it would lead her to true peace.

Once the modifications were made, Artemisa made her way back to the airport, worry starting to set.

The next flight wasn't for eight hours. Artemisa let out a heavy sigh as she purchased her ticket. Eight hours in an airport meant her risk of being spotted, caught by facial recognition, or noticed by police increased dramatically.

She sat on the floor, despite there being seats available. She firmed her back up against the wall and began to meditate, as she was taught. Artemisa needed to formulate a plan and she couldn't do that in her current state of panic and worry.

Meditation worked to an extent, but Artemisa needed her other coping mechanisms in order to deal with the airport stress. So she headed to one of the bars in the airport, saving the battery in her Gameboy for the flight.

Mercifully, she boarded the plane and took a deep sigh of relief. Like the flight out of the U.S., if she had been spotted, they would have moved before she had boarded the plane.

'*By mastering my emotions, I master the damage I cause*', Artemisa thought during the safety announcements.

When the plane was finally airborne and the stewards and stewardesses were bringing drinks around, Artemisa ordered a few drinks and enquired if there was a scrap of paper she could borrow. The steward obliged.

Her plan formulation was beginning to take fruition and on the piece of paper she wrote:

C.I.A. Agent Humpfrey Spencer

MI5 Agent Anthony Houghton

Polunin Yurievich

Magaldi Crime Family

They were the stones preventing her from achieving the tranquillity and peace she deserved and craved so much. The killing was the easy part and Artemisa knew that if the long probing fingers of the C.I.A. were out of the way, the killing of the others would be a more manageable task.

The names stuck in her mind more visibly now than when Artemisa had first read them in her file. Each one had played a part in her being where she was now, what she was, and she would be damned if any of them lived.

Killing the people on the list would be far easier than actually getting to the people. Artemisa had not formulated much of a plan, she conceded, but then again, coming to Japan had not been much of a plan either and yet it had helped. All the file had contained was the names of the people involved, not their current locations; that was the leg work Artemisa would have to perform herself.

The only plan she could think of on the flight from Osaka to Washington D.C. meant she was calling in the last favour she had, from the only person aware of her existence in the U.S. who did not want her dead, she hoped.

Once Artemisa was through the airport, she headed into the city. The last time she was in Washington D.C. was when she was nine, and it was to kill the aide of a member of congress. That had been an easy mission but didn't leave a lot of time for exploring the city.

Artemisa found a hotel with vacancies and collapsed gratefully onto the pillows, and was asleep before she could even get under the covers. The wake-up call from the hotel desk woke her with a start at five o'clock the next morning, and Artemisa sank into the bath, exhausted.

She allowed herself a soak to regain some of the lost energy before eventually getting dressed and heading out with the early commuters.

Chapter Ten:

At six-thirty that morning, she arrived at a coffee shop where she was greeted by an attractive, yet bleary-eyed barista behind the counter.

Artemisa ordered a cup of tea and waited politely for it to be made.

"Anything else?" she asked, stifling a yawn.

"Yes, can I buy a large black coffee with two shots of espresso for a regular, for when they come to pick it up later this morning, it's for Hannah Eckles."

"Yeah, we can put that through."

"Excellent, I'm their sister and want to surprise them," Artemisa said brightly.

She put the order through. Artemisa took a seat in the corner of the shop and drank her tea, grateful for the caffeine giving the boost she desperately needed. The coffee shop gradually filled with people stopping for a coffee before heading to work, and the take-out queue was soon out of the door.

Artemisa didn't know whether or not Hannah was in the U.S. at this moment or if they still frequented this coffee shop, which Hannah had only mentioned in passing when gaining Artemisa's trust.

Finally, Artemisa saw Hannah walk in, dressed in an

expensive suit, sharp heels, and their hair in a high ponytail with a briefcase clasped in one hand.

Hannah had seemingly moved up in the world since they and Artemisa had last spoken.

She could see the barista explaining to Hannah that their drink had been paid for, and saw out of the corner of her eye the woman pointing to her through the crowd.

A few minutes later, Hannah sat down across the table from Artemisa, "Hello sister," they said after a long sip of coffee.

Artemisa couldn't read Hannah's expression; it seemed to be an equal mix of surprise and annoyance. "Forgive the white lie but you're welcome for the coffee."

"Thanks. You look like utter shit," Hannah cracked a small smile, which settled Artemisa's nerves.

"Life, uh, finds a way of doing that to you."

"Why are you here?" Hannah asked, cutting all pretence.

"I'm tired of running, I'm tired of people being sent after me, I am tired of having to kill everyone sent after me. I want the location of Agent Humphrey Spence."

"Have you really thought this through?" Hannah asked, raising an eyebrow.

"Spencer, Houghton, Yurievich, Magaldi crime family are

going to die and then I am going to rest, not constantly look over my shoulder, I can be at peace."

"The Magaldi crime family?! That's who you got involved with? Jesus fucking Christ, Artemisa! What the fuck were you thinking?"

"I made a series of bad decisions," Artemisa replied bluntly. "The now deceased Richard Cherry has to take partial blame, as he got me involved with them. Then it led to Ashton Potter chasing me, who is now also dead. We really should have caught up."

"I suspected you may have had a hand in Richard getting run over after falling into traffic. So why are you sitting in front of me now, what do you need from me?"

"Agent Spencer."

"What about him?"

"I have left him very clear instructions to leave me alone, very clear messages. So I want to have a little chat with him. Magaldi decided to let the C.I.A. aware I was still alive after I left his employment. I thought he would take the hint. He has not."

"So you need his location?"

"Yes, and any file on me, gone."

"Why should I help?"

"Because I believe you want me to find peace. If you didn't, you wouldn't have helped in South Africa. You went through far too much to let me die." Artemisa let silence take over before she said, "You would benefit with him being out of the picture... and we both know what would happen if I reached across the table."

Hannah withdrew their hands from the table and clutched their thighs nervously before eventually saying, "You make some compelling points."

"I do, think about that promotion."

"If I do this, no more favours, no more help?"

"You'll never hear from me or see me again," Artemisa promised, her breath quickening.

"I'll get in contact once I have the information."

"Text this number," Artemisa said, sliding a number across the table.

Hannah put the number into their briefcase and stood up. Artemisa stood as well.

"Hannah," Artemisa said gently. "Don't fuck me over." It was not a threat, just more of a reminder.

Hannah nodded and bid Artemisa good day before heading out to work.

"Now we wait," Artemisa said to the empty chair in front

of her.

After draining the last of her cup of tea, Artemisa left the coffee shop. There was still no guarantee that Hannah wouldn't turn on her, but Artemisa was confident they had enough self-preservation and determination in order to help her.

Artemisa spent most of her day following tourist groups around the tourist sites in Washington. The more time she spent in crowds, the more comfortable she would feel, and the less likely it was for her to be picked up by security cameras or facial recognition. The thought of staying locked in her hotel room right now was unbearable.

It took eight hours for Hannah to get in contact with Artemisa.

"This Friday, Director Humpfrey Spencer will be hosting a poker night at his home with several other C.I.A. directors, if you want him then that is your opportunity," Hannah whispered.

"Can you text me the address?" Artemisa asked, her heart pounding.

"I hope you find peace," Hannah said, hanging up the call.

Artemisa scribbled the address down on a piece of paper and then disposed of the mobile phone on her way to the hotel.

When she returned to the hotel room, she checked the clock and what day of the week it was. *'Tuesday, I have time to plan',* Artemisa thought.

The C.I.A. provided her with means and opportunity to have several bank accounts in different countries with different names, so money wasn't a problem for her. But all banks were heavily secured and filled with cameras, so it was better to frequent them as few times as possible. Artemisa had to be clinical until this leg of the mission was complete, then it would be smooth sailing.

Artemisa spent the next day purchasing new clothes, as well as some running equipment. She returned to the hotel shortly after and let out a deep sigh. She fucking hated crowds, but it kept her busy; constant moving felt like progress, and sitting idle felt like she was waiting for another knock at a hotel door.

On Thursday, Artemisa got the train to a stop close to that of the now director, Spencer. She was dressed in her running gear and began exercising around the neighbourhood, surveying the house as she did laps.

The house was surrounded by high hedges, with a gated driveway. This meant she had one way in and one way out of the property. The house's security camera connected directly to the overhead cabling on the telephone pole. It took four laps for Artemisa to get the name of the security company that was hooked directly to the internet.

Once she was back in the hotel, Artemisa used the hotel's

computer lounge to do some research into the security company; all their cameras were internet-dependent and none were battery back-up. Artemisa let out a sigh of relief, that meant that her plan, as feeble as it was, was in fact possible.

Friday morning, Artemisa headed to a sports shop and bought a serrated hunting knife with no questions asked. "America is broken," she muttered to herself leaving the shop, tucking the knife into her jeans, under her t-shirt.

Back at the Hotel, Artemisa realised that she had two different options; the first being that she could go to Spencer's house now and be there for him when he arrived home. The second was waiting for Spencer to be in the property and then break in, meaning she lost the element of surprise.

Chapter Eleven:

After a long time mulling it over, Artemisa decided that it was worth losing the element of surprise, so she decided that she would wait to see how many people would be in the property when she entered.

So, at four o'clock that evening, Artemisa sat on a cold, hard bench, ready and waiting. She could see the house but could not be seen by the property she was scouting. Artemisa sat cross-legged, meditating, blocking out the distractions as Monk Ryo had taught her, as darkness approached and began to engulf her.

Eventually she saw three cars approach the house and Artemisa, under cover of darkness, approached the house as the gates opened and the cars drove inside.

As the gates closed and people began to exit their cars, Artemisa saw the bald head, plump physique and sweaty body of the man who had haunted her dreams for months.

She sat down again, and waited for the poker game to start. Artemisa sat shivering for 45 minutes before she put the next stage of her plan into action.

She scaled the telephone pole very carefully and cut the internet and security camera cables to Director Spencer's house. From the elevated position she could see a light on the camera blink off and remain off.

Artemisa vaulted the gate with ease before she scrambled in a crouched position behind a car. She waited, unsure of how aggressive she needed to be.

There were at least four people in the property, she saw those enter from the three cars. As Artemisa crouched, she saw the front door open and a woman appear in the doorway, looking into the still night, then up to the security camera.

As the woman turned, Artemisa made her move. She put one hand over her mouth to muffle a scream, as she put the woman in a sleeper hold. When she felt the woman go unconscious, Artemisa released the hold and gently placed her by the front door, which she then locked. She wasn't going to kill anyone who didn't deserve it.

The house was lavish as Artemisa looked around. She could hear voices coming from one of the back rooms. She heard Humpfrey Spencer's voice and felt her skin crawl.

"Honey, what has happened to the internet? We cannot play poker without our poker playlist," he called out.

Artemisa walked towards his voice, her heart beating fast and anger starting to rise. She opened the door and said, "Fuck off, Spencer." Crossing the threshold, she closed the door behind her.

All four men leapt to their feet, startled and shocked by her abrupt introduction. Humpfrey Spencer retreated into a corner as the others stared aghast at Artemisa.

One of the men ran directly at her, brave but incredibly stupid. She shifted her weight, and using his momentum threw him over her shoulder to the ground. She placed one of her feet on his knee, grabbed his foot and lifted it with all her strength whilst all her weight was on his knee, until the entire room heard the sickening sound of bone breaking.

"Sit down," she commanded.

"What did you do to my wife?" Spencer shouted.

"She is alive, now sit the fuck down and she'll stay that way," Artemisa explained calmly.

Director Spencer sat quivering in his chair as the man who had charged her lay whimpering on the ground, clutching his leg.

"Was my note at the airport hotel not enough? Or any of the other notes I have left you? Why could you not leave me alone? The bodies I left, the body of Ashton Potter?" Artemisa asked, looking directly at the director who was unable to make eye contact.

"You were an asset, to this country, to democracy."

"Shut the fuck up," Artemisa warned.

"You are invaluable to this country," he continued, ignoring Artemisa's warning.

"Don't fill me with your false propaganda, you don't believe it. Why could you not have let me live?"

"You believed everything you were doing was the right thing to do, then you got selfish."

Artemisa walked to one of the men who was huddled in the corner. She grabbed him by the shirt and dragged him into Director Spencer's eyeline.

She held his face for 15 seconds before letting go. His body crumpled to the floor and Director Spencer let out a terrified scream.

"When you found out I was alive, you should have kept it buried, yet you decided to try bringing me back to the fold," Artemisa said. "Why could you not have got the hint? How many bodies will it take? How many people will you need to read into classified files for you to realise I am not worth it?"

"Some things are more important," he said. "You belong to the U.S. government."

Artemisa said nothing, but walked over to the other man and threw a punch which connected with the man's head. He fell to the floor dead, and Director Spencer let out another terrified whimper.

"You brought this on yourself," she said calmly. "You've only got one more C.I.A. friend left, better think real hard about how you speak about me."

"Let me live," he begged. "I was nice to you, the others-"

He didn't get to finish the lie before Artemisa punched the man whose leg she broke, and he stopped crying; in fact, he stopped doing anything all together.

"Spare my wife," he begged.

"Does she know about me?" Artemisa asked.

"No."

"Then think of your wife, grow some fucking balls and accept your fate."

Director Spencer began to sob, but he didn't move.

"Do you remember what you did to me when I cried?" Artemisa asked. "What the army did to me? What the C.I.A. did to me as a scared, defenceless child?"

He sobbed even harder.

"You disgust me," Artemisa muttered, grabbing his face.

She made him look into her eyes as he died; the years of abuse, evil personified, were now dead in her hands.

She took his mobile from his pocket, disconnected the phone security and began deleting everything off his work computer via remote access.

As Artemisa left the house, she noticed that Director Spencer and his friends were about to drink an incredibly expensive bottle of whiskey. Given that they now had no need for it, she took it with her as she left the property.

She returned to the hotel to change, collect her things, and headed to the airport.

The next available flight was in five hours, so Artemisa headed to the airport bar. As she sat with a drink, a news story broke on the TV. Artemisa and the other patrons watched as they reported that a small fire had broken out at the C.I.A. headquarters in Langley.

When fire crews were on the scene, Artemisa raised her glass and toasted the television, and whispered, "To your promotion, Hannah."

The red-eye flight to London was a quiet one, but as with all air travel, Artemisa was unable to sleep, so instead she read a book she had bought at the airport with minimal interest. Her mind wandered after a short while and she wondered what would happen in London, and how much easier her missions would be if she had a plan.

Midway through the flight, she remembered her list,

~~C.I.A. Agent Humpfrey Spencer~~

MI5 Agent Anthony Houghton

Polunin Yurievich

Magaldi Crime Family

She crossed out the name of Humpfrey Spencer with a sense of accomplishment, before tucking the piece of paper away back inside her bag, and took out the Gameboy. Now the C.I.A. were off her back, the cat and mouse games had finished, and she could murder in relative peace.

Chapter Twelve:

When Artemisa cleared airport security, she headed towards a bank for a cash withdrawal and then to find a hotel. Once Artemisa had found and checked into the hotel, she slumped exhausted into the hotel bath.

"In hindsight, I should have gotten some information from Director Spencer before I killed him," Artemisa muttered to the bubbles, as she soaked in the water.

As Artemisa fended off the urge to go from the bath to the comfy, plush bed, she began to formulate the beginnings of a plan.

Artemisa eventually forced herself from the warm confines of the bath, changed, and headed down to the hotel's free-to-use computers; her only hope was that Anthony Houghton, like most people, had a social media presence that was exploitable.

She looked at the bars and pubs around the MI5 headquarters, to see if he had been tagged in any photos or posts. She had been a baby the last time that she had met Anthony Houghton, so she had no true memories of him. However, before her escape from the C.I.A., and with the aid of Hannah in South Africa, she had seen a more recent photo of the man, so that was the reference to go on. The file was locked in a safety deposit box in New York, so it was her memory or bust.

She spent hours at the computer, searching social media

and the internet for any crumb of evidence of his location, house or even a bar that he frequented.

After five hours of scouring the internet, she finally had a lead. Anthony Houghton had a wife and a daughter. His wife, Eliza Houghton, had inconsistent privacy settings on her social media accounts and Artemisa was able to find that once a month or so she frequented a cafe-bar hybrid on the other side of the city from Artemisa's hotel called 'The Cool Dinosaur Movement'.

Artemisa had time, she had a little patience and she wasn't working on a budget, so if it took a month or two, she had a lead that she could follow until another, better lead came about. The most important thing was the C.I.A. were finished with her and Hannah would not expose Artemisa.

On her way to The Cool Dinosaur Movement, Artemisa stopped at a bookstore. If she was going to stake out at this cafe for what could be upwards of a month, she might as well entertain herself whilst she did.

She found a table that gave her a good view of the entire place, set her books and MP3 player on the table and joined the queue to place an order from the bar.

Artemisa looked around at everyone, none of them looked like Eliza Houghton, but she wasn't expecting them to. They were groups of young mothers socialising, and a few tables of families; thankfully none of the children or babies were sat near her table.

Artemisa ordered a pot of tea from the waitress who gave her the most dazzling smile Artemisa had ever received and took her pot of tea and cup back to her table.

After another quick survey of everyone who was currently sitting down, she opened the book on the top of her pile and began to read.

"What is the book about?" a voice asked her.

Artemisa looked up to see the waitress who had served her, still wearing a wide smile, place a small pot of milk and some sugar down on the table in front of her.

"According to the cover, lesbian space necromancers, apparently," Artemisa said, returning the smile. She couldn't not, it was an infectious smile.

"You'll have to let me know if it is worth reading."

"I'll give you a full recommendation," Artemisa promised, still smiling wide.

Artemisa watched her go back to the bar, temporarily stunned. She was a head smaller than Artemisa, with black frizzy hair and her smile was genuinely infectious, purple lipstick contrasting beautifully with her skin. Artemisa could tell a fake smile from a genuine smile, and she was wearing a genuine smile with everyone she spoke to.

Artemisa eventually returned to her book, after being aware how long she was looking at her, but thought that drinking here whilst staking out Eliza Houghton would have its advantages.

Eventually Artemisa conceded defeat, and with tiredness kicking in she returned to her hotel, desperate for some sleep; it was with great effort that Artemisa forced herself under the covers, but once she was wrapped up she fell asleep instantly.

Artemisa's wakeup call at six o'clock that morning was not a welcome one. She yawned and stretched herself into her running gear before heading out into the early morning cloud. After pushing herself to run just over six kilometres, she returned to the hotel and spent an hour reacquainting herself with the weights. Not having access to a gym whilst in a Buddhist temple in Kyoto, she had not been as committed to working out as she previously was.

Artemisa showered, changed, picked up her backpack full of books and headed back towards The Cool Dinosaur Movement, desperate for some breakfast.

A full English breakfast with extra hash browns and extra bacon being delivered by the same smiling waitress as yesterday, was a welcome sight for Artemisa's tired eyes.

"Was my tea really that good? It made you want to return?" she asked, putting the breakfast down in front of Artemisa.

"Best pot of tea I've ever had," Artemisa chuckled, "you are to tea what Machiavelli was to philosophy," she continued, putting her book down to the side.

"I'm flattered. Sure you're going to be able to manage all of that?" she pointed at the plate.

"I've ran six kilometres and had a gym session this morning, I've earnt a big breakfast," Artemisa chuckled.

"Enjoy, I'll be over with your tea in a minute."

Artemisa devoured everything on the plate in what felt like seconds, and after surveying everyone who was currently in the café, went back to the book she started yesterday.

Periodically she would look up, but nobody had a close resemblance to Eliza Houghton.

Artemisa put the book down after reading the final page and stretched her arms out, subconsciously flexing as she stretched. When she looked back up, it was to find the waitress with the dazzling smile and a shorter, younger waiter both looking at her. Artemisa smiled and did it again, flexing for a little longer the second time.

After people were watching a bit more, she dived into the backpack and picked out another book.

"Was the first book worth reading or a don't bother?" Artemisa looked up into the face of the waitress, smiling at her.

"Worth it. I'm only sad I can't read the sequel as it isn't

out yet. Thankfully this book is the start of a completed trilogy," indicating the new books next to her.

"That is good! As you've given me a recommendation, once the lunchtime rush is over, I'll write a few recommendations for you, if you just plan on spending your days here reading."

"That is how I plan on spending my days," Artemisa said, a smile cracking across her face.

"I'll bring it over once the rush has finished then."

Artemisa looked round at the lunchtime rush. No Eliza Houghton, but a lot of interesting-looking characters. She had been trained to recognise non-verbal tells, mannerisms, ticks and what they commonly associated with.

She saw the signs of people who had recently given up smoking and were craving that one cigarette to calm them; those who were definitely hiding something from their significant others, by how they checked their phones, yet nobody who looked like they were married to a member of the British Secret Service.

As she watched, her eyes kept falling on the waitress who was juggling four different things at the same time. Artemisa couldn't imagine working with members of the public, she would definitely kill someone on her first day. But the warmth the waitress was showing was something Artemisa only experienced in a few places in New York.

The waitress was intoxicating. Artemisa watched her subtly make a baby giggle, her dungarees complementing the dark purple lipstick, and Artemisa couldn't help but want to look at her smile forever.

Artemisa had never had the time or the opportunity to establish and try out relationships, was never allowed to have personal feelings or explore her own sexuality. Given her upbringing and how easily she could kill people, it wasn't wise for her to kiss people, but the beauty, welcoming smile and kindness this frizzy-haired waitress was showing her was something she had never experienced before. And she wasn't mad about it either, Artemisa thought back to her time in New York and realised that she may have been flirted with, whether she recognised it or not.

When the lunchtime rush was over, she walked over and pointed to the seat opposite Artemisa, saying, "Do you mind if I take this seat?"

"Be my guest," Artemisa said, shutting the book and placing it on the table.

"I don't think I properly introduced myself. I'm Lily."

Artemisa paused, unsure whether to give her real name or use an alias, but she decided on being honest with Lily. "I'm Artemisa, and you have a name as pretty as your smile."

"Very kind of you, Artemisa. Is that an Italian name?

Greek? Your accent isn't that of an Italian and Greek, but not British. It is an enigma to me. Working this job, I'm normally good with accents, everyone from everywhere comes in here."

"I am an enigma," Artemisa said with a sly wink. "I was born in the U.K., but have kinda travelled and lived here, there and everywhere really."

"I am envious that you've travelled, I really want to travel," Lily admitted.

"Do it."

"Just like that?"

"Just like that. Book your flights, go to an airport, pack four days' worth of clothes and go."

"What about work?"

"I can tell you like your job, nobody can fake a smile like yours, but one thing I've learnt is that there is always another job available. Someone will always want to get drunk, someone will always need help getting someone drunk. If your money starts running low when you're travelling, then find another job."

"What about my flat?" Lily said, a glint in her eye.

"Do you get on with your parents?"

"I do with my mum but not my dad."

"Do they have a spare room?" Lily nodded. "There you go, sell the flat, move into that room and there is your travel and flight money."

"A smart brain behind the muscles, tattoos, and pretty face. I like your simplistic take on it."

Artemisa blushed slightly, but was spared trying to find a reply by Lily needing to rush off to tend to a customer at the bar.

Artemisa watched Lily making the customer's coffee, and for the briefest moment wondered if that is what she would have been like, if she had not been born in the circumstances that she was. But Artemisa knew, deep down, she was the person she was because of her past, because of everything she had been through, and that version of herself would not be the Artemisa that she would recognise.

"Will you still be here in two hours?" Lily asked Artemisa, a short time later. "I'll be finished, and we could always grab a drink?"

There was no sign of Eliza Houghton. She was not being chased by the C.I.A., so Artemisa didn't need to think too much about the answer she gave.

Two hours later, Lily was leading Artemisa through the streets of London, toward a cocktail bar.

"What are you going to order?" Lily asked, as they

perused the menu.

"I honestly don't think I've ever had a cocktail, so you may have to order for me."

"How have you never had a cocktail?" Lily asked, an incredulous look on her gorgeous face.

"Just been more of a cider or a whiskey and coke kinda girl, and not had the chance to frequent too many cocktail bars, my former jobs didn't allow too much freedom."

"I'll order for you, then," Lily announced, getting up from their table and heading to the bar.

Lily returned with drinks, as Artemisa looked into her face and cracked another smile, something she was not used to doing. "So, tell me about yourself?"

"Oh, I'm fairly boring," Lily said, which Artemisa did not believe. "Just finished university, the café is just a full-time job for me to build up my bank balance, before I look for another one."

"What did you study?"

"Philosophy and international relations with a master's in ethics."

"So not only are you a good person, you've spent the past four years learning how to make other people good people."

171

"Wouldn't say that," Lily said modestly.

"You would have liked my old employer. They were a big fan of quoting Bentham to justify whatever they wanted," Artemisa said, taking a sip of the drink Lily had bought for her.

"Greatest good for the greatest number of people," Lily rolled her eyes.

"Exactly."

"What made you want to study all that?" Artemisa's interest definitely piqued.

"My family loved discussing their political opinions and their ethics. I spent most of the time disagreeing with them, so I wanted to put some basis behind my disagreements and to infuriate them further."

"Spite is the best motivator, I bet they love arguing with you now!"

"My father ends up throwing his toys out of the pram. What about you, Artemisa the enigma, you've not revealed too much about yourself?"

"Flew in from the States to do some touristy stuff, drink tea in cafés, have a few alcoholic drinks. Before, I worked in the U.S., went to Japan, but wasn't there for too long, not as long as I wanted, before having to head back to the U.S."

"Parents? Siblings?"

"Never met them, probably dead. Siblings are doubtful," Artemisa shrugged, quickly realising this was a dark thing to say, so hastily apologised.

"No need to be sorry, I wish I was as independent as you."

"Still a mama's gal at heart?"

"Something like that," Lily said vaguely. "How is your cocktail?"

"Delicious, whiskey based?"

"Yeah, it's called 'Old Fashioned'."

"It's lovely, what is in yours?" Artemisa asked, looking at the fruity-looking drink.

Lily angled the glass round and swung the straw in Artemisa's direction.

She tried it and let out an involuntary shudder; it was a lot sweeter than she had imagined, but she had to accept that it was not at all unpleasant.

"Think I'll stick to the whiskey-based ones, but it isn't awful by any means."

"How long are you planning on staying in London?" Lily asked.

"As long as I need to be. If you're happy in a location, then why move on? I won't be returning to my old job so let's see what happens when the tide changes and the moon shines bright."

"I like that answer."

"What about you? You said the café is a stop-gap on your path to bigger and better things. What are bigger and better things for you?"

"I... I am at a roadblock."

"What kind of a roadblock? In my experience, a sledgehammer and pry bar are the easiest methods of destroying concrete."

"This is more of a parental roadblock."

"I'm sure you could still use a sledgehammer and pry bar." Artemisa laughed before saying, "Your mum or dad?"

"Dad."

"Well, two brains are better than one, let's find a way around it," she said, collecting their empty glasses and heading to the bar to order the new drinks.

When Artemisa returned to the table with fresh cocktails, Lily was not in the scheming mood. So Artemisa quickly changed the topic by saying, "I have no idea if these cocktails are any good, but they were 2-4-1 so I've gotten us four."

"What is yours?" Lily asked, looking at the drink.

"It's called a 'Miss Lynch': shot of tequila, shot of rum, a lot of fire whiskey, ginger ale or cola. Served with a cinnamon stick," Artemisa said, "Yours is a 'Horny Hangover': bourbon, black Sambuca, Jägermeister, spiced rum, peach schnapps, and Amaretto. They asked if you wanted it with cranberry juice, Coke or lemonade. I got them to do the one they recommend."

"And those two?" Lily asked.

"'Strap-On': gin: tequila, schnapps, absinthe, vodka with either Coke, lemonade or tonic. This one is with tonic," Artemisa explained, before convincing Lily to tell her stories about Lily's adventures at university.

Artemisa listened intently, thriving on the stories, a life that could have been. She enjoyed listening to the stories and Lily seemingly enjoyed having a captive audience.

Once their drinks were empty, Lily let out a yawn and said, "Will I be seeing you tomorrow?"

"Would you like to see me tomorrow?" Artemisa said, answering the question with a question.

"You're good to have around, I suppose," Lily said coolly.

"Then I will be around," Artemisa said cheerfully.

"Then I will see you tomorrow, Artemisa," Lily bid her goodnight.

Artemisa watched her companion into her taxi before making her way back to the hotel.

The next morning after her wake-up call, Artemisa pushed herself to do an eight-kilometre run, as she was having a furious internal argument. On the one hand, her past and training was reminding her to focus on the mission, and not allow any distractions in the way of her main focus. However, she was also being honest in that there was no sign of Eliza Houghton, so why not take some time to explore the world around her as opposed to being laser-focused. Letting people in was human and she needed to teach herself that she was a human and not just a killing machine.

This internal argument continued in the gym, in the shower and on the underground towards The Cool Dinosaur Movement. Once she had taken her seat, ordered a large breakfast and seen Lily, she knew which side of the argument had won.

Artemisa fell into a nice routine over the next four weeks. She didn't spend too much time in the café when Lily wasn't in and although there was no sighting of Eliza Houghton, despite Artemisa stalking her social media on the regular, Artemisa wasn't that concerned; she was smiling more than she ever had previously.

The C.I.A. now not being a concern was a weight off Artemisa's shoulders. She couldn't quite believe it made her yearn ever so slightly to be back in New York, enjoying the city again; her meditation allowed her to cope better and this city was comfortable.

Lily was finishing early on the last Friday of the month, and she and Artemisa were having a well-earned alcoholic beverage. Artemisa, at ease for the first time in a long time, looked around the café as Lily talked to her about her other regular patrons, until her smile slid off her face.

"What's wrong?" Artemisa asked, suspicious that this was a rare occasion where Lily wasn't smiling.

"I told my mother not to come here for business meetings, she always tries to get drinks on the house in order to impress people. I'll be 30 seconds."

"No worries, I'm going to the bathroom," Artemisa said, getting up and walking in the opposite direction.

When Artemisa returned from the bathroom, she could almost see the steam rising from Lily, based on her expression as she stood at their table talking to her mother.

Artemisa froze, an abyss of despair forming in her stomach, followed by a rapid panic, and an overwhelming sense of sadness and fear. Lily was talking to Eliza Houghton. WHY did she not think to ask Lily her last name? The first thing in Artemisa's mind was to run.

Artemisa didn't know if she could leave without saying a word. Did she owe Lily an explanation? Artemisa didn't know as she walked over, trembling.

As she approached Lily, she felt the words come out of her mouth and she said, "I've got to go, I've not been honest with you."

She and Lily froze, as they came to the realisation that they both said the same thing at the same time.

"Let's walk," Lily said slowly, handing Artemisa her full pint now in a take-away cup.

Artemisa had no alternative but to take the cup from Lily and follow.

"It's my dad," Lily sighed, after walking in silence for 10 minutes.

"I know, that is why I need to speak first," Artemisa said, looking straight ahead.

"What do you mean? What do you know about my dad?"

"He works for British intelligence, M.I.5. Twenty or so years ago, he was called to a Manchester-based hospital where a baby killed whoever was holding it when it cried or got emotional, which for a baby happened quite frequently. They quickly learnt that when this baby was emotional, it could drain the life out of anyone it came into contact with; killing them quickly. Anthony Houghton sold the child to the C.I.A. as part of a diplomatic agreement, so the C.I.A. could run test experiments on the child and also groom the child into being a living weapon and child soldier," Artemisa said grimly.

"How do you know this?" Lily asked slowly.

"Because, I have had to be real careful about my urge to hold your hand when you've been sat across the table from me."

"Wait, did you travel to London to kill my dad? Was everything you told me a lie?"

"No, my previous job was in security. I wouldn't lie to you, but that is an oversimplification. I was on the run from the Americans, and I was beginning to lose my control over what I do. So that is when I headed to Japan to learn how to control; I went there to learn meditation, inner peace, to control all that shit. However, the Americans were still after me. The monks made me realise that whilst they were after me, whilst the people who knew what I could do were still after me that I could never be safe, I could never find peace."

"The reason me and my dad don't get along is that I found out about everything he did," Lily said, stopping to look at Artemisa. "I was 13, maybe 14 and I went into my dad's office to leave my school reports on his desk, when I saw his computer was unlocked, I was curious so I began to look through it... The things I saw were horrific, there were details about you, and everything he had done in the years before and after that. I confronted him, it changed everything."

"So you knew all his secrets?" Artemisa asked. "You even knew about me?"

Lily took a step closer and lightly took Artemisa's hand. Artemisa took a deep breath, focusing on ensuring she did not harm Lily.

"Remember what I said over cocktails about those family roadblocks?" Lily said, moving an inch closer.

Artemisa nodded.

"I tried to expose everything I had seen. I got in contact with a journalist, next thing I know, he goes missing. I go to university, top of every class, and yet I can't get a job in any field. Even after being offered the job in an interview, the offer is withdrawn after. He has been sabotaging me, stopping me from doing the right thing. Maybe helping you is the right thing to do."

"That's why you hate him?"

"That is why I hate him."

Artemisa felt Lily wrap her arms around her in a hug and she remembered to focus on her breathing as Lily said, "Let's get out of the cold and back at your hotel, we can talk about this tomorrow, let's not spoil the night."

"I would think that is the last thing you would want," Artemisa said.

All she could smell was Lily's perfume, inhaling it as if it were oxygen. Her breathing was deep and heavy.

"It's okay, open your eyes," Lily whispered.

On command, Artemisa opened her eyes and allowed Lily to lead her, holding her hand gently.

She led Artemisa around the shops and then back to Artemisa's hotel. Once they were sitting comfortably on the bed, Lily explained what her mum said to her back at the café.

"My father will be back in the country tomorrow," Lily replied.

Artemisa poured whiskey into her glass, drained it, and refilled it again before she spoke. "Are you sure you understood me when we were stood outside?"

"Your quest for peace and your hit list, yes I was listening to you. Out of interest, how exactly did you get involved with a crime family?"

"After I escaped the services of the C.I.A., I was excitable, naïve, innocent. Unsure if they believed that I was truly dead. I was anxious, had no plan, limited access initially to the funds I stole. They offered me employment, safety, immunity and family; turns out they were just using me the same as the C.I.A. were."

"They got annoyed when you wanted out?"

"No, not really," Artemisa sighed. "They got furious."

"So, what is the plan? Once your hit list is completed?"

Artemisa thought about this, swilling her drink around in its cup. "I would buy a wardrobe full of clothes, a nice house. Live out the rest of my days."

"What?" Lily said, letting out a slight laugh.

"All my life I've bought clothes when I've needed them, thrown them away when they needed washing and then moved on, never having time or a place to keep them. I've lived out of backpacks. It would be nice to own my own clothes, wash them and keep them. It would be nice to walk into a room and not pick up vantage points, escape options, exposed ligaments, and ways to break people."

"You need rest."

"I do need rest. However, this is not the time to rest, as we need to address the elephant in the room."

"The fact that I am in your hotel room, despite you stating that you're going to kill my dad, and you came to London to do so."

"Yes."

"Look, you're on your own path. We both are on the same mission, regarding my father. I tried to expose him, ruin him based on the things I have seen him do. You're here to kill him. Both outcomes mean he doesn't get to hurt people any longer."

Artemisa didn't say anything. Mulling this over it made sense, but she didn't know how Lily was truly feeling about it.

"You're also on a warpath, your vengeance will stop for nobody, all I ask is you allow me to get answers from him."

"I understand," Artemisa said eventually.

"Also, the way I am starting to feel, I think that staying at your side is the right thing to do."

"I've never really not been alone before, I would welcome some company," Artemisa said, after a long pause.

"Good, let's go over the plan," Lily said confidently.

"Wait, we have a plan?"

"How are you still alive?" Lily asked incredulously.

"God's sins outweigh my own, he will never come for me," Artemisa shrugged. "I figured that makes me invincible."

Although Artemisa had no plan, it was still better than Lily's plan to invite him round for tea.

"What then? You have a dead body in your flat?" Artemisa joked sarcastically.

Lily mulled this over, before saying, "Kill him in public?"

"We would be spotted, London has too many CCTV cameras."

"Then his home."

"Won't your mum be there?" Artemisa asked.

"Fuck, we could invite her out to dinner, then be late?"

"Won't that be suspicious that you invite her out on the first day he is back in the country?"

"I mean, no matter how we do this, she is going to be upset her husband is dead."

They sat pondering in silence before Lily eventually suggested, "Knock my mum out."

"I was trying to avoid hurting her physically."

"By the time she wakes up, we can be in Russia," Lily said.

Artemisa looked at Lily, her drink inches away from her lips. "We?"

"I'm in this for the long haul, your quest for peace isn't one you need to do alone anymore."

Artemisa didn't say anything.

"Besides, you're killing my father."

"That is a good point," Artemisa said. "Won't your mum be wanting to see you, be with her, mourn with her?"

"Doubtful, she has her friends. She knows my thoughts on him and his on me, and if we are already on holiday she will understand."

"I am sorry," Artemisa said simply.

"I know, but the day after tomorrow is a day sooner to peace. But anyway, it's getting late," Lily said, turning on the television.

"It *is* getting late," Artemisa yawned.

"Come relax and lie down," Lily said, inviting Artemisa to lie on her own hotel bed.

Artemisa moved from the chair to the bed.

Lily moved Artemisa's drink from her right hand to her left hand and moved her right hand and put it around her, nestling herself contently.

Artemisa shuddered and took a deep breath.

"You don't need to be scared," Lily said.

"I don't want to kill you."

"I don't want you to do that either, and you won't kill me, I promise."

Artemisa smiled.

"I don't suppose you get a lot of time to watch movies."

"My former employer was called Roman Magaldi. One of Magaldi's fronts was a movie theatre, they used it for money laundering, so I spent some time there."

"Did you get any downtime?"

"Kind of, but looking back everything was designed to draw me into the fold. When I joined it was days after I escaped the C.I.A.; I went from sitting in movie theatres to killing on his behalf."

"So you didn't really have much time to do your own thing... or date?" Lily asked, her voice a little higher.

"No, it's also difficult to date when you need to be constantly worried about not killing someone; making sure you keep your heart rate steady, emotions in check, scared a prolonged touch means that someone is about to die."

"Can you feel it? When someone died?"

Artemisa nodded solemnly.

Lily said nothing, instead she was running her fingers over Artemisa's tattoos, looking at them with great interest.

"What even is this film?" Artemisa said, curiously.

"Not sure, I'm not really paying attention," Lily said, kissing Artemisa on the cheek.

Artemisa went hot and bright red in the face, and felt a smile spread across her face.

"You look nice when you smile," Lily said, her voice low.

Artemisa turned her head to face Lily. She looked into Lily's face until Lily said, "I get you are new to this, but this is the part where you kiss me, you fucking idiot."

When Artemisa awoke it was to find a note from Lily saying, 'be back soon x'.

Artemisa got up and sank into the bath. When she eventually got out of the bath, it was to find Lily sitting on the bed.

"You woke early."

"Yeah, sunlight from the curtains was right in my eyes. I have something for you."

"What is it?" Artemisa asked, looking up from her shoelaces.

"This," Lily said, throwing a box to Artemisa. "It is a watch, it will tell you your heart rate, pulse, blood pressure, so we know when you're safe and when you need to meditate and take a deep breath."

"Thank you," Artemisa said, unboxing it and allowing Lily to strap it to her wrist.

"This way, we both stay alive," Lily said, planting a gentle kiss on Artemisa's cheek.

"Are you sure you want to do this?" Artemisa asked.

"Yes, I get the answers I need, I get the future I want, and you get the peace you need."

"If you want to back out, change your mind or change the plan-"

"I'll say so," Lily finished, before Artemisa could get the words out.

They packed their bags and left the hotel.

"My dad will spend most of the day de-briefing before eventually returning home," Lily whispered to her, so other people on the Tube could not hear, and because nothing annoyed Londoners more than people speaking on public transport.

Artemisa nodded, the rings on her fingers being spun and as the uneasy feeling began to rise.

"Passports and flights are booked," Lily said, her voice quiet.

"Glad you are organised," Artemisa laughed.

Lily led Artemisa quietly.

"Go into the garden, I'll signal you," Lily whispered.

Artemisa sat on the ground behind the door, waiting for Lily to give her the all-clear.

"Mum is in the kitchen, Dad is in his study. Let's go."

Artemisa crept into the kitchen. Eliza Houghton did not hear a sound, as Artemisa put her in a tight chokehold, and once she was out like a light, Artemisa lifted her up and carried her into a bedroom and placed her down on the bed.

When she arrived downstairs again, she nodded to Lily who called out, "Dad, are you home?"

"Lily, this is a surprise," he said, exiting his study and not sounding surprised or happy to be hearing from his daughter. "Who is this?"

"You probably don't recognise me? I am Artemisa. I was only a baby when you stole me from a Manchester hospital."

He froze, and Artemisa noticed his eyes shift to the door.

"Don't run, just answer Lily's questions and accept your fate," Artemisa quipped in a bored, monotone voice.

"What questions could you possibly have?"

The question was a sneer and Artemisa resisted the urge to strike him.

"Did you have the journalist killed? If it was me, would you have sold me to the C.I.A.?" Lily asked.

"Yes."

The reply came almost instantly. There was no hesitation,

and no remorse. Lily nodded and walked past Artemisa.

Artemisa sat opposite him and sighed deeply.

"You think this will change anything? You think you'll be able to rest, live a normal life?"

"Maybe not, but I am going to enjoy this and I must say, you're taking it better than Director Spencer of the C.I.A.; he died like a little bitch."

Artemisa let this sit in the open before grabbing him by the throat.

"This cannot change anything, not after everything you've done," he croaked.

When Artemisa let go of his throat, he was a dead piece of shit. She let him fall to the floor.

"You were a lot of things, including a shit father, nobody will miss you," Artemisa said to the dead body in front of her.

Lily was outside. She was pale and there was an unreadable expression on her face. Lily didn't notice Artemisa until she was wrapped in her arms.

"I'm sorry," Artemisa whispered.

"He deserved it," Lily sniffed, "Let's go."

Artemisa held Lily's hand tightly, not wanting to let go, until her heart rate was getting dangerously close to 200, so she reluctantly released.

As they sat on the Tube towards the airport, Artemisa said, in vain, "Last chance to turn around."

"Babe, I am not turning around," Lily replied, defiantly. "Let's get through airport security and get a drink."

When they both had a pint in their hands with a shot chaser, Lily said, "To the old fucker."

They clinked glasses and drank deeply.

"Have you thought about how you're going to explain your holidays to your mum?"

"We went for drinks last month, I'll say I told her then," Lily shrugged.

"How are you feeling? Honestly?"

"I don't know. Honestly, it's weird, I should be feeling emotions, but I am just empty, it's hard letting go of all the resentment, the anger, everything."

"Letting go will take time, and you don't need to go through anything alone."

They continued drinking until their boarding flight was called and they made their way onto the plane.

"I'm getting sick of flying," Artemisa grumbled, as they listened to the safety announcement.

"At least once we are back in the U.S., we will be there a while, no more flights."

"One day we will travel for pleasure and not just for business," Artemisa vowed.

Chapter Thirteen:

As the plane began taxiing to the runway, Lily began squeezing Artemisa's fingers, causing her rings to cut into her skin as she tightened her grip, but Artemisa didn't object or make an attempt to stop her.

Lily fell asleep quickly, nestled in Artemisa's shoulder. Artemisa sat wide awake next to her, unable to sleep, trying to read her book with one hand.

She was uneasy about how they would be treated in Russia and was mentally steadying herself for what could be a turbulent trip. As Artemisa was thinking this, the plane started to judder and Artemisa prayed it was not an omen. The turbulence awoke Lily and she restarted squeezing Artemisa's hand.

"I need a drink, do you want or need anything?" Artemisa asked, unbuckling her belt.

"Don't leave," Lily muttered. "Please."

"It's alright," Artemisa reassured her, sitting back down.

Lily was relieved when they eventually landed. She was not a keen flyer, that much was evident.

"Sure you're okay, Lily flower?" Artemisa asked, as they queued to leave the plane.

"Yeah, that turbulence just fucked me up a bit."

"You're alright," Artemisa said, squeezing her hand. "You hungry?"

"Famished, need food and a shower."

"Both will be provided for you," a voice said from behind them.

They turned to see a short, plump man with a thick moustache staring at them. Artemisa moved slightly so Lily was shielded.

"Artemisa and friend, this way," he instructed.

Lily waited for Artemisa to move and followed, staying on her heel. She noticed Artemisa's right hand was clenched in a fist. They walked for 15 minutes, until they entered a conference room and were offered seats.

"I don't suppose time zones really matter to you, given that you look like shit" he said, pouring vodka into three glasses, placing one on a coaster in front of him and offering the other two to Artemisa and Lily.

"I suppose they don't matter," Artemisa said, but she did not drink.

"Good, I don't like drinking alone, it has been a stressful few hours," he said, taking a sip.

"Because of my arrival?" Artemisa asked, taking a sip now she had seen him drink.

"Yes, I want to ask you a question, will you answer it honestly?"

"Of course," Artemisa said.

"Are you here to kill Polunin Yurievich?"

Artemisa drained her glass and waited for it to be refilled before she answered, "Yes, yes I am."

"Thank you for your honesty," he said, before turning to one of the men who had accompanied them into the room. "Sergie, get a car ready for her."

"Wait, you're going to take me to him and let me kill him?" Artemisa said, unsure as to whether she had heard properly.

"You have killed a C.I.A. director, set a fire in Langley to destroy all evidence of your existence. You have killed the M.I.5 agent who sold you to the C.I.A. Now you are here in Moscow. You want to disappear after the C.I.A. were made aware of your re-existence. We want you away from Russian soil. This will work out best for all parties involved."

"So, I kill him, leave here, never return and you're happy with that?"

"Correct."

"Can you book us flights to Boston then?"

"It will be taken care of whilst Sergie takes you to Polunin Yurievich, will your friend be staying here?"

"No, she will be coming with me," Artemisa said coolly.

Artemisa and Lily followed Sergie in his sharp suit out of the airport towards a car.

"How do you know this isn't a trap?" Lily whispered.

"None of them were armed, but we don't."

Sergie began to drive in silence, Artemisa and Lily sat in the back of the car in silence.

After about ten minutes, Sergie said, "So you can drain the life out of people and kill people with a punch. Must be hard to control."

"Yeah."

"Shame, must make petting dogs very difficult."

"It does, I need to be careful," Artemisa replied, surprised at the direction the conversation was going.

"I would not like being unable to pet my dogs."

"That wouldn't be nice."

"Truth be told, most people will not be sorry to see Yurievich dead. The KGB should have killed him a long time ago and when the KGB became the FSB, he still should have been killed."

"He was outbid by the C.I.A., for a killer baby," Artemisa laughed.

"Yes, yes he was. Either way there is no difference in the fact that you helped destabilise half the world, and did as you were ordered; who gave the orders made little difference."

"That is an interesting point," Artemisa said, thinking about this deeply.

"I always make good points; it's why I was chosen to drive you."

"What other wisdom do you have?"

"He will put up a fight, the old bastard will not go down easy."

"I wouldn't expect him to die crying."

"If it is okay, I would like to see you fight."

"You may get the chance to."

The rest of the drive was in remote silence. Artemisa was calmer than she was expecting. Lily looked nervous and Artemisa did her best to reassure her that there was nothing to worry about.

Artemisa handed Lily her MP3 player and reassured her again nothing was going to go wrong, as Sergie parked the car.

Sergie and Artemisa walked up a driveway towards a front door with peeling paint. Artemisa stood back, as Sergie knocked the brass knocker.

The door was eventually opened by a mountain of a man, with a thick, unkempt, grey beard. He made Artemisa look petite and unable to lift the lightest weight.

"He looks like a fucking tough bastard," Artemisa muttered to Sergie.

"I am a fucking tough bastard," the man growled.

"Good," Artemisa said, almost relishing the fight.

"The government supports this?" he asked, turning to Sergie.

Sergie nodded in response.

"So be it," he muttered, turning and walking into his house, allowing Artemisa and Sergie to follow him. He walked into an open living room, clearly favouring one leg over the other.

"Let's see if little girl can kill me," he said, taking a swig from a bottle on the table.

Artemisa was ready; her rings and jacket were in the car with Lily, and she was ready for a fight.

He charged at Artemisa, who was prepared for this, but he had the size, weight and strength advantage. Artemisa crouched, making her centre of gravity as low as possible. She grabbed him below his knee and attempted to drive him upwards as one of his fists connected with her ribs.

He drove his other knee into the side of Artemisa's head as he fell backward. She scrambled to her knees and launched a punch with her left hand, as he did the same.

Both fists connected, Artemisa's fist connected with his temple and his connected with her jaw. For the sake of Artemisa's jaw, he did not move as her head began to spin.

She lay her back on the floor for a moment, her jaw and her ribs screaming out in agony. "He packs a fucking punch," Artemisa groaned after a few moments, clutching her head with one hand and her ribs with the other.

"He is now dead, you are not," Sergie said, from against the wall.

Artemisa staggered to her feet, and Sergie carefully grabbed her shoulder as Artemisa swayed.

"Are you okay?" he asked.

Artemisa nodded and accepted Sergie's help getting her back to the car. They left without a backwards glance at the tough bastard, who despite managing to get a few blows in, now lay dead, alone in his house. Once in the car, Sergie began to drive as if what he witnessed was perfectly normal. None of them said anything for 20 minutes. She eventually said, "I don't think I've ever been punched like that."

"You won't need to again," Lily reassured her, patting her hand gently.

Sergie agreed with this.

The drive back to the airport was quiet, as Artemisa was dizzy, so she sat contently her head on Lily's shoulder.

"We have delayed a flight so it will be more convenient for you," Sergie said. "So you can shower and eat before boarding."

"Thank you," Artemisa said, massaging her jaw.

Once they had eaten and showered, Sergie led them through the airport, where the short, plump man was standing, waiting for them again.

"Good to see you back again," he said, leading them towards a boarding gate.

"Thank you, Mr Sokolov," Artemisa said, still rubbing her jaw where she could feel a bruise forming.

"Russia bids you farewell, Artemisa," he handed over a bottle of premium vodka.

"I thank Russia for its hospitality and generosity," she said, accepting the bottle and leading Lily towards the tourists who were boarding the plane.

Chapter Fourteen:

As the safety announcements were being explained, Artemisa took Lily's hand and lifted it to her lips, kissing it multiple times.

"You softy," Lily laughed.

Artemisa nodded but didn't say anything, her head spinning. As soon as the seatbelt sign was switched off, Artemisa ordered a drink, lifted the armrest and wrapped Lily in her arms, kissing her gently on the cheek.

Lily checked Artemisa's heart rate before nestling into her arms and falling asleep. Artemisa, for the first time in memory, began to doze on an airplane, with Lily wrapped in her arms.

They were woken up by one of the air stewards, when it was time to land.

"Are we heading directly to New York?" Lily asked sleepily.

"Nah, we will stay in Boston for a night or two," Artemisa replied, attempting to stifle a yawn.

"Why?"

"I'm hungry, I need a shower and I need to plan."

"You're going to plan?" Lily asked, surprised.

"We are going to need to."

They cleared the airport security and began looking for hotels. Once they found one, Lily collapsed onto the bed and Artemisa ran a bath.

With the water running, Artemisa took the list out of her jacket pocket.

~~C.I.A. Agent Humpfrey Spencer~~

~~MI5 Agent Anthony Houghton~~

~~Polunin Yurievich~~

Magaldi Crime Family

After updating the list, she put it back in her jacket pocket and went to sink into the bath. She closed her eyes and let the water warm her. When she next opened her eyes, it was to see Lily with her mobile to her ear listening to her voicemails and talking to her mum.

When Lily got off the phone, Artemisa got out of the bath and wrapped herself in a towel, trying not to drip water all over. Artemisa asked, "Are you okay?"

"Yeah, I set my voicemail to say I was on this holiday as well, she apologised for not remembering and informed me about my father's death. She wasn't begging for me to return, which is okay."

"Are you going to be okay?" Artemisa repeated.

"I will be after a bath, some food and a good night's

sleep."

"Well, when you're in the bath let's order room service," Artemisa suggested, picking up a menu.

Once the food arrived, Lily asked, "Why are we suddenly planning? You flew to London with no plan, and we flew to Russia with no plans."

"This is different," Artemisa said, swallowing her food without chewing and subsequently coughing. "This isn't killing one person, this is about dismantling an entire organisation."

"Is that what you need to do?"

"Yes, I helped build the Magaldi crime family to what it is now, I am not going to allow it to remain. The things I did for them rivalled the things I did for the C.I.A."

"Why not kill him and leave? Why destroy it all?"

"Magaldi saw a vulnerable nineteen-year-old, who never had a family before. Manipulated me in the same way the C.I.A. did, used me to establish their empire, I was their instrument of death in a bloody coup. They opted for the carrot as opposed to the stick."

"How long were you with them?"

"Over a year."

"Well now it is all about your progression."

Artemisa nodded.

"Do we have a plan for tomorrow?" Lily asked, as they finished their food.

"Get some new clothes and then begin planning."

"Can you afford new clothes?" Lily queried nervously.

"I have multiple accounts of stolen C.I.A. and crime family money that they don't know is missing, under different names for security. Once this is all over, we don't need to worry about money."

"That makes sense, if they don't know they're missing it, then they can't be mad at you using it."

"Exactly, I consider it my wages backdated."

The next morning, they left the hotel heading towards a shopping mall. Lily was excited about going to a mall for some shopping.

"Remember, we travel light." Artemisa smirked, as Lily's eyes lit up at the amount of shops there were.

Artemisa got everything she needed quickly, but Lily wanted to try different clothes on, even the ones she was not planning on buying.

"You're going to need to make a decision quick, my heart rate is going up," Artemisa said, tapping her watch, as Lily looked stunning in every single thing she tried on.

"My apologies," Lily said, in a tone suggesting she was not sorry at all.

"Shall we stay another night?" Artemisa asked, as they walked from shop to shop.

"How come?"

"It's a four-hour train journey and I am really sick of travelling," Artemisa sighed.

"Then we will stay another night," Lily agreed simply.

They returned to the hotel room, turned on the TV and Artemisa wrapped Lily up in her arms, taking deep breaths as she did so. After a while, Lily eventually asked, "When you left the Magaldi crime family, is this how you saw your life going?"

"You in my arms? No, not by a long shot. What about you? When I first sat down in the café, did you see this?"

"Did I think when you walked in, you would be a trained killer, there to stalk my mum to murder my dad? No, definitely no. Did I think I'd be in your arms, yes. I made sure the others wouldn't flirt with you and made it my goal to be wrapped up in your arms."

"You bullied them, so only you could flirt with me? That is so sweet," Artemisa chuckled.

"Who would have thought that the most dangerous woman on the planet would be such a softie."

Despite waking up refreshed and in a good mood, when they eventually took their seats on the train from Boston to New York, Artemisa knew it would be a long four hours, when they began listening to the other people who were on the train.

"Don't let the knobheads annoy you," Lily whispered, watching Artemisa's eyes glare at the group of balding men discussing their political opinions in loud voices.

Artemisa let out a sigh and attempted to return to the book she was reading. As the train trundled along, though, it wasn't just Artemisa who was annoyed at the group of men, other passengers were throwing them disgruntled looks.

"You fucking lot are what's wrong with this country," one of them said at the top of his voice.

Artemisa's eyes flicked up from the page and saw the group he was talking to. She sighed. Lily watched Artemisa check her heart rate at 138; she had some breathing room away from the dangerous 200.

Artemisa stood up, and she could feel the eyes of the carriage on her as she said, "Leave the women alone."

"What the fuck do you want?" the man said at her.

"I want you to shut the fuck up and sit down. You little fucking bitch."

"What, are you offended? Snowflake fuck, this is our

country. Fuck you."

"Not offended, and it isn't really your country, is it?" Artemisa laughed, taking a step forward.

"You fucking abomination, how dare you!" he screamed upon seeing that Lily was sitting next to Artemisa.

Artemisa was almost willing him to say something to make her retaliate; she was almost daring him to do it, as she was at the end of her tether. Lily, however, was not up for Artemisa fighting as much as Artemisa was, and she took a hold of Artemisa's wrists.

Other passengers put their arms out as well, stopping Artemisa from walking forward. The man, as angry as he was, still had a trace of fear in his eyes as Artemisa stood glaring at him.

"Sit down and shut the fuck up for the rest of the journey," Artemisa said.

The man paused. It seemed to be taking his brain a long time to either formulate a sentence or figure out whether or not he thought he could beat Artemisa in a fight.

Eventually he sat back down and Artemisa followed suit, sitting back next to Lily.

"They're being escorted off the train at the next stop," the passenger who put their arm out to stop Artemisa, said to her.

"Good," Artemisa scowled.

"Relax," Lily whispered.

"I'm calm," Artemisa growled through gritted teeth, showing her the watch screen.

"You're tense."

Artemisa's fight or flight response was set firmly on fight, her fists remaining clenched, until they arrived at Grand Central Station. They walked out into the concrete jungle.

Artemisa led Lily through the city, walking past the tourist focal points on the way to a hotel. Lily absorbed the tourist sites as they walked, and Artemisa made a mental note for them to visit them, as tourists, as opposed to just walking past them.

They checked into a hotel and flopped down onto the bed. Even though it had only been a four-hour train, it felt like they had been travelling all day.

"Get to formulating a plan," Lily yawned.

"I am," Artemisa yawned.

"Good, glad you're not just going in with no plan."

"Going in with no plan led me to you," Artemisa reasoned.

Later that evening, they made their way down to the hotel bar, for some food and drinks.

"Let's hear the plan," Lily said, once they collected their drinks from the bar and headed to the corner of the room.

"Start off by taking out some of the lower-level guys; disrupting the money flow, re-distributing the money accordingly, then work the way up the food chain. Act as though this is a coup, a power play, as opposed to total dismantling."

"Why not just schedule a meeting with Magaldi?"

"Killing him wouldn't do anything. He's a snake, you cut off one head and two more grow in its place. I am going to destroy his empire."

"That... that isn't how snakes work," Lily said, eyebrow raised. "You know that, right? I need to know if you know that."

"Yeah, but it's a saying."

"You're definitely not saying it right."

"The point is still apt," Artemisa reasoned. "I'm destroying the empire I helped build and everyone with it. I'm not just going to allow someone to take his place. He made the mistake of allowing me unfiltered access to his entire organisation. I sat in bars listening to people talk to each other about their roles within his organisation; it helped manipulate me, made me feel more comfortable within the business. It will allow me to bring it crumbling down."

"When do we start?"

"Woah, woah, woah, babe. You're gonna spend the days being a tourist, trying New York pizza. I'm keeping you as safe as possible, and having you help take out the Magaldi crime family is the opposite of 'safe as possible'. You'll help when it comes to redistribution of money."

Lily paused, before saying, "I don't want to be alone."

"For the first time in my life, I'm not alone," Artemisa confessed, cupping Lily's hands in hers. "I am going to keep it that way, I promise you won't be alone, but you will be safe. I will only leave your side when I have to."

"Promise?"

"I promise, besides you've got the most important job," Artemisa said, after taking a sip of her drink.

Lily tilted her head, unsure whether Artemisa was being genuine or not.

"We are stopping Magaldi's cash flow, but we cannot allow that money to go on anything illegal. Meaning, we are gonna have a load of cash. The amounts would be suspicious if we walked into a bank to deposit the money, meaning it'll need spending. Waitresses will need tipping very generous amounts, you'll be changing their lives. Buy some nice clothes, get them sent somewhere for when this is all over. Think of the New York shopping district and you with unlimited money."

Lily smiled at this, as Artemisa said, "Think how beautiful

you'll look in all of the jewellery."

"Alright, you've convinced me," Lily said, smiling.

Chapter Fifteen:

When Artemisa awoke the next morning, it was early, and sunlight was baking the carpet with a warm glow. Lily was still asleep, so she slipped into her clothes, and after leaving Lily a note, tiptoed out of the hotel room.

She walked to a local bodega and bought two cheap phones, supplies, and then stopped for some fresh bagels, returning to the hotel room before Lily had woken up. When Lily did wake, it was to find Artemisa agitated, her legs bouncing more than they normally did, and drumming her fingers on the notepad in front of her.

"You weren't this agitated before, what's wrong?" Lily asked.

"Magaldi is different," Artemisa muttered. "Spencer made the C.I.A. and the U.S. military fill me full of propaganda, a false sense of pride and duty, a sense I was making a difference to the entire world. Magaldi wants power, control, unquestioning respect, and money. I have no issues with anything I've done or what I did, but Spencer was never on missions, he sat in an office. I remember the look in Magaldi's eye when he watched me kill, it made my skin crawl then and it does now."

Lily looked queasy and Artemisa stopped talking.

"As long as you're going to remain safe," Lily said, eventually.

"For you, I would not let death stop me."

"Good. Are those fresh bagels?"

"Yeah, I nipped out whilst you were still sleeping."

"Why didn't you wake me?"

"You looked peaceful," Artemisa admitted honestly.

"Oh, to have breakfast in bed as your beautiful girlfriend plans murder and revenge," Lily laughed. "I think the time zones knocked me out."

"Why not spend today in bed then. Nap, watch TV, order room service, I am only a text or call away," Artemisa said, throwing the phone onto the bed next to Lily.

"Are you gonna be alright without me?" Lily asked.

"If you eat and rest then yes, I'll be okay," Artemisa replied, giving her a gentle kiss before leaving.

In the elevator, Artemisa checked her scraps of paper for who her first targets would be. She decided she would take out two lower-level intimidators. Their jobs were simple, intimidating business owners so they would take protection from the Magaldi family.

Artemisa had frequented multiple bars with Ruffo Molton and Ezo Tumlin before and they were fucking idiots. She didn't trust them to secure the protection deal; they intimidated and left.

She couldn't kill the entire crime family in one day, it was impossible. She couldn't get to them all one go, so instead she would just pick them off piece by piece.

Artemisa got off the subway and headed towards a bank. She accessed the safety deposit box she kept there and withdrew a small notebook and a stylish flip knife, which she put in her boot. After checking her notebook, she headed towards a coffee shop the two idiots used to sit in until they get their orders.

When she arrived, she saw the lumbering, gormless men exactly where she expected them, in the coffee shop, basking in the early morning sun. They were waiting, so Artemisa did the same; she sat waiting for them to make a move.

She spent her time texting Lily, reassuring her that she was in no harm. It took 45 minutes for the lumbering goons to move. When they did, Artemisa let out a groan. They were accompanying Gio Magaldi; he was a high roller cousin of Magaldi, and Artemisa did not expect him to be using the services of Ruffo and Ezo.

Artemisa kept her distance but followed them. She had a theory about where they were going but she hoped she was wrong; she did not expect her plan to be moving this swiftly. As Artemisa dodged around a pram and angry mother, she reasoned that even unexpected situations had the chance to be profitable.

Artemisa's concerns turned out to be accurate, as Gio

Magaldi was heading to one of three tattoo parlours owned by the Magaldi family. Cash-only businesses were the best fronts for money laundering; only one of the three parlours was any good and this was not one of them. It was not the one Artemisa had had her tattoos done at, this one was garbage.

She saw Gio follow the *artist*, who she only knew as Max, into the back as Ruffo and Ezo sat down on the sofas in the waiting area. Artemisa took off her rings, slipping them into her pockets as she crossed the street.

She took a deep, steadying breath and opened the door. It took her four steps to be in front of Ruffo, and she swung a punch towards him. Before he looked up, she connected with his temple, and using the momentum from the punch she span and leapt towards Ezo, who was now looking up. Her right hand met his throat as her left punched him in the face.

Artemisa straightened up, and looked at the two now-dead men, positioned where they were before she entered the parlour. Artemisa vaulted the small barrier to the back of the shop where the tattoo chairs sat empty. She headed to the door at the back of the room; it was time for Gio and Max to meet their fate.

She crouched, listening intently to the conversation that was happening behind the door. Ironically, they were discussing funeral arrangements, but neither of them mentioned a name of who was either about to die or had recently died.

As Artemisa was contemplating how best to make her next move, she heard Max say, "Wait here, sir, I will get the diary of an incoming shipment."

Artemisa held her breath as the door opened, and Max stepped out. Once the door swung shut, she waited for Max to get a notebook from his desk. As soon as he picked it up, Artemisa pounced. She covered his mouth with one hand, and with the other she began to squeeze his throat. He flapped his arms for a few seconds before he became limp.

Artemisa heaved him into a tattoo chair, took the notebook from Max's limp fingers and put it in her pocket.

Artemisa regained her position behind the door, waiting for Gio to get impatient and come to look for Max. It didn't take long. Gio burst out of the room, only to come face to face with Artemisa, sitting there smiling at him.

She kicked him hard in the chest and he staggered back into the room. Artemisa followed, closing the door behind her, and she punched him hard in the face, shattering his nose.

She took his mobile, using his fingerprints to disable all security features, put the phone into airplane mode and then turned it off. If she needed it, this way it couldn't be tracked.

She used Gio and Max's fingers to open the safes and emptied them out into black duffle bags which sat in the corner of the room. She carried four duffle bags out of the tattoo parlour and made her way down the street.

She walked for 20 minutes before hailing a taxi and going straight back to the hotel, and back to Lily. Artemisa wanted to make sure Lily was okay; she didn't like the thought of leaving her alone for too long. As the taxi sat in traffic, Artemisa began to panic. She put her rings back on and began playing with them. She was anxious; she did not know what to do in a relationship, what if she messed it up? She kills the girl's father, then accidentally breaks her heart or does something wrong, what then? Destroyed the girl's life.

Artemisa tried to meditate in the taxi, push these thoughts from her mind, nothing was going to go wrong. Artemisa was determined to do this, she was unsure what had brought these fears on but she ignored them, just wanting to get back to the hotel quickly. She began compulsively texting Lily, assuring her that they were both okay and both safe.

Eventually, Artemisa hauled the duffle bags into their hotel room and dumped them on the floor. It was a little after two o'clock when Artemisa arrived back; Lily was still asleep, face buried into the pillow. Artemisa's texts were unread and Lily unaffected and calm.

Artemisa didn't disturb her. Instead, she began looking

through the notebook she took from Max and the phone she took from Gio. Careful not to take the phone out of airplane mode and ensuring it was offline, she didn't want to alert Magaldi until it was time. She also wasn't keen on killing someone so close to him, so early into her dismantling of his empire.

She noted down the time, date and locations of everything of note, most of it was money drops at the tattoo parlour and the amounts of money that would be dropped.

Artemisa looked up as Lily awoke and stretched deeply, looking around the room. Lily smiled as she saw Artemisa sitting there.

"You're so fucking cute when you snore," Artemisa said, as Lily grinned.

"Shut up," Lily yawned, launching a pillow across the room.

"How are you feeling?" Artemisa asked.

"I'm really hungry," Lily groaned.

"You feeling up to going out for food, or want me to bring you food in bed?"

"As much as that sounds nice, let's go out for food," Lily said, hopping out of bed and heading towards the shower. "What's in the bags?"

"Money," Artemisa said, unzipping one of the bags and showing Lily the stacks of notes in there.

Lily's eyes widened, "The clothes, the make-up, the jewellery I could buy with that."

"You'll get the chance to spend some of it," Artemisa smiled, "we just need to get it to an amount where it isn't suspicious for me to deposit into various bank accounts."

When Lily was in the shower, Artemisa counted the cash that was in front of her. In each bag, she estimated there was a minimum of 80,000 dollars; the issue for Artemisa was they were all stacks of one hundred-dollar bills.

Walking into the bank with 80,000 dollars in one-hundred-dollar bills would be a sure-fire way to arouse suspicion. As Lily was showering, Artemisa tried to imagine what reasoning she could give to a bank teller for depositing such large deposits of cash - the best she could come up with was casino winnings.

Artemisa and Lily walked into a nice-looking steak house and sat down, Lily looking radiant and Artemisa beginning to panic.

"You can relax," Lily assured her.

"I am relaxed, I'm just not a fan of having people in my blind spots," Artemisa, shuddered.

"Once we're finished here, you'll never need to be concerned again," Lily replied, optimistically.

"I hope so," Artemisa said; it was a nice fantasy but she doubted the realism of the dream, she had seen and done too much to ever fully let her guard down.

As they ordered their steaks, they began discussing different options or ideas as to how to make just under 400,000 dollars in one-hundred-dollar bills, non-suspiciously.

"How many bank accounts do you have in the U.S.?" Lily asked.

"Four."

"So we can deposit some money in those, then why not set up a new bank account to deposit the money in?"

"It's a good idea, doesn't get around the questions they would ask. It's the anti-money-laundering laws that we need to get around."

"What if you faked an invoice from a casino and then paid the cash into each bank that way."

"I don't think there is a way to do it legitimately," Artemisa sighed.

"If there is a way then we'll find it," Lily said, leaving a 380-dollar tip as they finished their food and moved over to the bar to continue their drinks.

"Have you thought any more about your plans when this is over?" Lily asked.

Artemisa took a moment to think about this before she shook her head saying, "I'll plan that once everything is over. What about you? You'll have no roadblocks, the world is your oyster."

"As long as I'm with you, I don't really care. What job I get is meaningless now."

"We'll see what happens," Artemisa said, raising her glass.

"Do you have any more work planned for this evening?"

"None, my evening is yours," Artemisa said, an uneasy feeling in her stomach.

Every part of her wanted to spend the rest of the day and night killing everyone that she needed to kill for her long nightmare to be over, but she knew it was fruitless and she would need to be patient.

Artemisa didn't sleep well that night. She tossed and turned before giving it up as a bad job. So as to not disturb Lily, she moved from the bed to the chair and began searching for ways around anti-money laundering laws.

She considered burning the money, showing Magaldi that this was personal, but by doing this it would just be painting in block capitals that it was her. Pretending that it was a rival or someone within his company would be the quietest way for committing murders of mafia members.

Artemisa researched this until five o'clock in the morning, when she decided it was time to exercise. So she changed into her kit and went for a seven kilometre run, before heading to the hotel gym for a weights session.

Lily joined her in the gym once she woke up, and they had a gentle workout.

Artemisa began showing Lily how the apparatus worked.

Lily asked, "Why are you so stressed? Everything is going to plan. Nothing will go wrong."

"Magaldi is different," Artemisa muttered.

"Perhaps once he realises who he is dealing with, then he'll organise a meeting, a ceasefire as it were."

"I would be as good as dead walking into that meeting, this is a delicate game of chess."

"Well, you need to be a few moves ahead, have leverage over him."

"What, like kidnapping his mother?" Artemisa laughed.

"I mean, would that work?" Lily asked seriously.

"Lily, I am not kidnapping his mother," Artemisa laughed, as they finished their workout and showered.

Lily asked about a plan for that day, as they went for breakfast.

"I am waiting for that tattoo parlour to open," Artemisa said subtly, nodding down the street.

"Why?"

"Because it is a front, and Fabio, Luca and Matteo are the three brothers who I need to have a meeting with."

They had third helpings of pancakes as they waited for the shop to open. When Artemisa saw the brothers arrive, she finished the rest of her pancake, kissed Lily on the cheek, and assured her she would be back soon.

Artemisa walked across the street, the taste of pancake and syrup still in her mouth as she opened the door to the parlour and surveyed the situation. One brother was sitting at the desk muttering to himself, another was prepping ink, and disturbing sounds were coming from the bathroom, which is where Artemisa guessed the third brother was.

She reached across the desk and grabbed Luca's hand, before he had truly realised what was happening. Once he was dead, she took the keys from the desk.

She locked the front door before she made her way behind the counter, heading towards Fabio. She laid his body on the bed and waited for Matteo to stop destroying the bathroom.

Once he was out, she pounced, before, in a bout of deja vu, she repeated the actions of the day before, putting all of the cash from the safes in the backroom into a bag, grabbing notebooks and leaving the shop.

Lily met her outside of the café and they headed back to the hotel, Artemisa keeping a tight grip on the backpack and a gentle grip of Lily's hand.

"How do you feel about strip clubs?" Artemisa asked, as they locked the door of their hotel room.

"Ethically, it is important to support sex workers and ensure that they are safe when they work, but I wouldn't say a strip club is up there on my date locations in New York; I'd prefer you take me to some tourist destinations first."

"I'm not taking you there on a date," Artemisa said, rolling her eyes. "We need to get rid of this money, I would estimate we have just over a million in one hundred-dollar bills here, we need it shifting."

Chapter Sixteen:

That afternoon they headed across the city towards Harlem, Artemisa leading the way and keeping the backpack with the money in very secure until they arrived.

"Club Cinnamon," Lily said, looking at the neon sign.

Artemisa nodded. "Club Cinnamon, we are here to meet Mr Cinnamon."

"That cannot be his name?" Lily said incredulously.

"No it's not, but that is what we will call him," Artemisa warned.

"I'll follow your lead," Lily said, as they entered the club.

It was dark and relatively empty; the music was loud and there were two stages with dancers on them.

Artemisa and Lily walked past the stages, towards the back office.

"This is a staff only area," a man said, blocking them from going any further.

"Mr Cinnamon is expecting me," Artemisa said, taking a step forward. "Tell him I am here, or he'll be hiring your replacement."

"Wait here," he said, his voice cracking, and he turned and went through the door.

"Is threatening him wise?" Lily whispered to Artemisa.

"It's fine, don't worry," Artemisa said confidently.

Sure enough, the man returned a few minutes later and said, "Mr Cinnamon is looking forward to seeing you."

They entered the back office to see a man sat behind the desk, looking at them with a keen expression on his face.

"Artemisa, good to see you! I heard you were dead," he said warmly. "You've brought a friend."

"I am unkillable. And no, I've brought business, how much business is up to you," Artemisa said.

"Take a seat," he gestured to the chairs on the other side of the desk.

Lily and Artemisa sat as Mr Cinnamon spoke to the man who was on security. "Marcus, bring three glasses, ice and the finest whiskey we have."

The man nodded and left the room, none of them spoke until he returned with glasses and a bottle of whiskey.

"So you are here to do business?" he asked, pouring them all a dram.

"I wouldn't go to anyone else."

"Because I am the best there is."

"Naturally, and discretion is key."

"What are you looking to do?"

"I need cash deposited into bank accounts without any questions being asked."

"How much are we talking?"

"Four bank accounts, splitting a million."

"I can see how you walking into a bank would arouse questions."

"It would indeed, what sort of cut would you be looking for?"

"Well that depends," he said slowly, and Artemisa was resisting the urge to complete this transaction by force.

"On what?"

"Do you have it in cash or assets?"

Artemisa paused before opening her backpack and showing him the contents.

"In that case, I'll take a 100,000 cut, and we can have the money in your bank account in minutes."

"In minutes?" Artemisa said.

"I can wire transfer you the money and keep the cash."

Artemisa looked at Lily, who nodded, and Artemisa, turning back to Mr Cinnamon, said, "Okay."

"Excellent, I see you have brought someone with brains, to match your brawn," Mr Cinnamon said, toasting his glass in Lily's direction.

They began counting all of the cash, it came to just above $1,600,000.

Mr Cinnamon allowed Artemisa to enter the bank details with anonymity.

"I do like it when you come and visit me," he said, as Artemisa sat back down. "Is your business in New York just starting, or at its grand conclusion?"

"Just getting started," Artemisa said, cautiously, not wanting to give too much away.

"Then I imagine this will not be the last time we complete business transactions."

"It will not be the last time, providing everybody forgets my face, forgets the fact I am in New York and forgets I am here on business."

"I understand. In your line of work, discretion is key, and you will have it from Mr Cinnamon."

"Thank you, and depending on how you play your cards, the fallout from my business may prove to be lucrative."

"Will you be a long-term business partner? I only ask because I may be losing another partner in the near future."

Artemisa paused, "People retiring is always unfortunate, but it is a part of life, don't dwell on it."

Artemisa drained her glass, and Lily thanked him, leaving her glass mostly untouched as they walked past Marcus again and left the club. The sunlight was dazzling in comparison to the club.

"So how do you know Mr Cinnamon?" Lily asked.

"He is a fence. I did some work with him when I was helping set up Magaldi's empire. He has always been a means to an end and there is no love lost between them."

"So it's safe to go to him?"

"We will see once we check if the money has gone into the accounts," Artemisa smiled.

"It's quite exhilarating seeing this side of the world," Lily said.

"Glad you're enjoying it," Artemisa chuckled.

"Do we have any other business to take care of?"

"Nope, we can do whatever you want," Artemisa said.

"Good," Lily said, taking Artemisa's hand.

They went to the various banks, and Artemisa checked her accounts before she and Lily spent the day exploring New York shops.

They had dinner and drinks back at the hotel and Artemisa sat there, drink in hand, smile on her face, across from Lily, thinking that if it weren't for the murders she had to commit, then this would be the closest thing to perfection that she could think of.

Artemisa and Lily both fell asleep quickly that night, but once again Artemisa could not stay asleep, and she awoke with a start at four o'clock.

So resigning herself to the fact that she would not be able to get back to sleep, she began formulating the next stage of her plan. Magaldi would notice six dead, including a family member, and over a million dollars missing in two days, which means he would start to move all cash to a central location and be on high alert. The police he owned in the city would also be on the same high alert.

This meant that if Artemisa was going to hit the cinema, she would need to do it that day. The issue with hitting the cinema was that it was a two-person job, and she didn't want to get Lily involved.

Artemisa looked across at the beautiful girl asleep in the hotel bed and let out a low groan. Artemisa once again began to worry about Lily's involvement in this. The fear of what could happen to Lily if it all went wrong was near crippling.

Once she hit the cinema, she would need to find out where all of Magaldi's cash was being consolidated, before she moved onto the higher members of the

Magaldi crime family and then finally Magaldi himself. Once she hit the cinema, it would also confirm to Magaldi that these were not just ordinary robberies, someone was after the Magaldi empire.

Artemisa looked over the notebooks she had collected from the tattoo parlours to see if any of them had a contingency plan written down for if the cash flow had to be diverted, but nobody was dumb enough to write it down.

When the time came, Artemisa went for another run and gym session and returned to the hotel room for Lily to wake up.

Once they had showered and were having breakfast, Lily asked for the day's plan and Artemisa had to make her decision quickly.

"The plan is risky," Artemisa muttered, as a waiter walked past.

"How is that any different from anything else you do?"

Artemisa thought this was a good point as she said, "Because this plan needs help, and I don't want to put you in any more danger."

"Tell me the plan. I'll decide whether or not it is too risky," Lily reasoned defiantly.

Artemisa doubted that Lily would actually say it was too risky, but nonetheless she explained her plan.

"I am confident we can pull this off, what is the worst that could go wrong?"

"We could both get killed," Artemisa said, "If I call it off, we sit and watch the film, deal?"

"Deal," Lily agreed.

Artemisa had misgivings as they sat on the subway, on the way to the cinema complex owned by Magaldi.

Artemisa's hand shook so badly it was making Lily's arm shake as they walked towards the cinema.

"This looks like an ordinary cinema," Lily said, as they approached the building.

"That is the point, it is a regular cinema," Artemisa smiled. "This way."

They walked around the back of the cinema and crouched down, waiting for the people who were on their smoke break to finish.

"Let's go," Artemisa whispered, leading Lily towards the wall. "See that black cable?"

"Yeah," Lily said, looking up at a cable running along the wall.

"Cut it," Artemisa instructed, handing her a knife. "Get on my shoulders."

"Okay," Lily said, breathlessly.

Artemisa crouched down as Lily clambered onto her shoulders.

"Ready?" Artemisa asked, standing up and holding onto Lily's ankles.

Within a minute, Lily had cut the wire and was back on the ground.

They walked casually into the cinema and queued for tickets, popcorn and drinks. Artemisa kept her head down low, wearing a cap and glasses. There was still a chance she would be recognised.

They made their way up the escalator towards their screen, Artemisa beginning to feel queasy.

"Lily, stand with your back and one leg against that wall, opposite the toilets. If anyone comes, then kick the wall subtly," Artemisa said, handing her the drinks.

Lily nodded and watched Artemisa continue on until she reached a staff-only door.

Artemisa cautiously tried the door handle, it was locked. She expected this, but was disappointed it was not easier for her. Using the knife, she managed to break the door hinge, shimmy the lock and enter the room.

Seven punches, seven dead, Artemisa had to act quickly in case she was interrupted. She downloaded everything she could onto a memory stick and poured a drink into the main ports of the computers and promptly began to destroy the equipment. She subtly left the room, re-joined Lily and they headed to their screen.

"In the clear?" Lily whispered, as they took their seats.

Artemisa nodded, trying to stop herself from shaking. Her heart was thumping against her rib cage. Staying in the cinema for the movie was not a smart move, but with how empty the cinema lobby was it would look suspicious if they turned and left again.

Artemisa's heart rate was dangerously high, and as the trailers started, Artemisa closed her eyes and began to breathe deeply.

Artemisa's mind drifted to her safety deposit box, and she thought about the amount of things she had on Magaldi. It would make very interesting reading if she handed it to the news reporter who had slipped Artemisa her card, all those months ago.

The film started and Artemisa tried to pay attention, but it was fruitless, she was too anxious to fully comprehend what was happening. She gently placed her fingers on Lily's hand, keeping her close as she steadied her breathing.

Forty-five minutes into the film, Artemisa knew that someone had discovered what had happened, as the fire alarm started, as did the sprinkler system.

They followed the couples and families also in the screen

out and towards the fire escapes.

"Keep your head down and walk fast," Artemisa urged.

They noticed an increase in security as they all left the building. Once they were outside, they continued walking for 20 minutes before Lily hailed down a taxi and got a ride back to the hotel.

When they arrived back at the hotel, Artemisa sank into a chair, put her head in between her legs and took deep steadying breaths as Lily ordered the drinks.

"It's alright," Lily said, soothingly rubbing Artemisa's back.

"I know," Artemisa whispered, "Thank you, baby."

Lily put a straw in Artemisa's pint and brought it in her mouth.

After drinking most of the pint through the straw, Artemisa looked up at Lily and said, "I'm good."

"I know," Lily said soothingly. "I know." She continued to rub Artemisa's back, not believing anything Artemisa said.

It was a few drinks later when Lily asked her, "So what was in the cinema?"

"Data, evidence, invoices, shell companies, holdings."

"All that was in the cinema? I'd expect more security."

"That was the back-up of everything, everything is in the

main offices."

"So you hit the back-ups, smart."

"Glad you think so," Artemisa said, smiling at her, with a grin so wide it made her face feel unnatural.

"So you're hoping to find where Magaldi will move the money to and steal it?"

"Nope, we're going to burn it."

"Burn it?"

"Every single dollar," Artemisa said, a glint in her eye. She initially dismissed the idea, but it seemed inevitable now the cinema was hit.

"Why?"

"It's too much cash to do anything with, so we are going to burn every single dollar."

"Explain to me how this works and why?" Lily said, confused.

"So Magaldi has businesses like the tattoo parlour, which is cash only. They say they have fifty customers a day, and they paid ten thousand dollars; that goes into the safe then into the bank."

"So Magaldi can put his illegal money through legitimate businesses?"

"Exactly, now he has a mixture of small businesses like the tattoo parlours to move small money, and he has shell companies and fake businesses to move large amounts of money."

"So with the small businesses now being robbed and you now having back-ups of everything, you think Magaldi will panic and move their cash to one central and secure location?"

"Exactly, if he thinks he is being robbed or that it is an inside job, then he will react."

After Artemisa's gym session that morning, she and Lily began going through everything on the memory stick.

"It's all here," Lily said, shocked. "Business names, holdings, owned properties."

"This would be enough to put him in jail for life," Artemisa said, "however, what we are looking for is warehouse listings."

"There are at least 20," Lily groaned.

"Then I guess we need to go exploring," Artemisa said.

She hired a car, went to a garage, filled up jerry cans full of petrol, and they drove, Lily in charge of the stereo and Artemisa remembering how much she hated New York traffic.

Sixteen warehouses were a bust, the 17th warehouse

looked promising.

"This is it," Artemisa said.

"How can you tell?" Lily asked.

"This is the only facility that has this much security," Artemisa noted, "Three cars, six people walking around the facility, heavily armed."

"Wait, you picked up all that?" Lily said, as Artemisa drove off again.

"Yeah, the question is, what do we do between now and nightfall?"

"Why nightfall?"

"Because I'm not going to take out three drivers, three passengers and six heavily armed mobsters before committing arson in daylight," Artemisa chuckled. "I am bold, but I am not that bold."

"Lunch then?" Lily suggested.

"Lunch. Then some touristy stuff," Artemisa said, realising how hungry she was.

Chapter Seventeen:

After lunch, Artemisa led Lily to the Empire State Building. They joined a queue of tourists and made their way through the historic building. Lily was excited and Artemisa was happy seeing how excited Lily was. As they walked the guided tour of the building, it made Artemisa feel normal.

Once the tour was over, they stood on the watchtower, overlooking the city and Lily let out a low whistle and said, "It's quite a view."

"It is," Artemisa said, looking at Lily as opposed to New York.

"You're not even looking," Lily said, turning her head.

"I am," Artemisa smiled.

From the Empire State Building, Artemisa and Lily headed to Times Square.

Artemisa suggested Grand Central Zoo, as the sheer number of people in Times Square was making her feel terrible. They spent most of their day there and it was calming for Artemisa to walk around looking at the animals.

As evening fell, Lily asked, "What time are we leaving?"

"We?"

"You'll need a lookout whilst you're taking out the cars and the armed guards, plus you'll need someone to help with the petrol pouring."

Lily had given this some thought and Artemisa groaned, not that the mission was impossible solo, but it would be easier with help. She took her time before saying, "Does it matter if I say no, or advise you to stay here?"

"Not really," Lily said, unfazed.

"Fine," Artemisa groaned.

Artemisa drove in silence, the anxious knot in her stomach not easing.

"First thing we need to do is verify the money is in there, after that we go from there."

"I thought all of the security confirmed it?"

"It was a good indicator, but I want visual confirmation."

"How do we get that?"

"We look through a window."

Forty-five minutes later, they received the visual confirmation. Getting on the roof of the warehouse next to the one owned by Magaldi was more difficult than getting confirmation. Cash was being offloaded from trucks and cars and stacked high.

"What now?" Lily whispered.

"We wait for them to finish unloading, I want it all burnt," Artemia muttered.

So they waited for almost two hours until the last car and van left. Artemisa made her move. The cars had rotated since this morning, but people sitting in parked cars opposite a warehouse at night was a sign of something suspicious.

Artemisa crouched behind the car door, listening to their conversation. Once they confirmed that there were only two people in the car, based on their conversation, Artemisa leapt up and swung her elbow into the passenger side window.

As glass sprayed across the passenger's lap she threw a punch at him, which connected with his temple. Artemisa, acting fast, dived through the shattered window and grabbed the driver as he made a move for his gun.

Artemisa took the gun from his body and made her way to the next car. She didn't want this to turn into a shootout, but having the firearm meant she didn't need to use her elbows to smash any more car windows.

She moved further down the street. Keeping low, she saw the passenger door open and heard a disgruntled man say, "Fucking dickhead, doesn't want me to smoke in the car."

Artemisa watched him light his cigarette and take a drag before she acted.

She reached out and grabbed the man's ankle, draining the life out of the man. He slumped back against the car as Artemisa waited to see what the driver of the car would do; the answer, as it turned out, was absolutely nothing.

He did not seem to notice that his companion was limp and not moving against the passenger door, so Artemisa walked round and opened the driver's side door and threw a punch as he looked around.

Once the third car had been dispatched, Artemisa crouched down, bouncing gently on her toes watching the armed guards patrol the perimeter.

One false move and she could get caught in a firefight, so she watched, waiting for one of them to break formation; they were not trained soldiers, they were stooges and soon enough one of them broke formation to go and answer nature's call behind a dumpster.

Artemisa moved in like an apex predator about to strike their prey. She waited for him to finish urinating and zip up his fly before she struck. She disarmed him and left him next to his urine.

One down, five to go. Artemisa waited, curious to see how they would act.

"Someone go check on him, see if he is taking a shit," a voice called out.

'This is almost too easy', Artemisa thought as she saw the

flashlight approaching the dumpster. She pounced, killing the man. Placing him next to the other, she turned off the flashlight and scurried to another position.

Two down, four to go. They were spread thin, and Artemisa knew it was time. She waited; they were patrolling in a clockwise fashion, which made it easier for her.

She ran, light on her toes, and launched a punch at the man who had just turned the corner. His head bounced off the wall and he slumped down, leaving a faint splatter of blood on the wall.

Three down, three to go. They would be around the corner momentarily. Artemisa heaved the last man to his feet and squared up behind him, using him as a human shield. As the next patroller walked around the corner, Artemisa pushed him forward.

The man instinctively caught his counterpart and before he could register the blood or Artemisa from behind him, his face became close acquaintances with Artemisa's fist.

Four down, two to go. Artemisa waited. They would come to her. Adults, whenever drawing a weapon, always point it at someone of a similar height. Artemisa crouched low, waiting for them to walk around the corner and spot the two bodies.

The high pitch yelp let out by the man as he walked around the corner was loud, but not loud enough to alert anyone else. After a brief struggle, she threw his body near the others.

Five down, one to go. Artemisa began to relax, and she waited for him to arrive. The hardest part was done, she just needed to move the bodies and then the real work began.

As he arrived, he let out a startled scream, louder than the previous scream. He threw punches as opposed to going for the gun on his waist. Artemisa was grateful for this, but the outcome either way would have been the same.

Artemisa moved all the bodies to the dumpster before leaving, re-joining Lily and they drove into the warehouse.

"This is more money than I have ever seen in my life," Lily said aghast, looking around at the mountain of money.

"I would be surprised if it wasn't." Artemisa laughed. "Most people won't have seen this much cash in one place. I haven't either, to be honest."

Artemisa began pouring the petrol from the jerry cans everywhere haphazardly and then proceeded to help Lily very carefully pour petrol over the cash.

Artemisa took a lighter out of her boot and after escorting Lily to a safe distance she lit the trail of petrol and stood back. Artemisa and Lily stood and watched the money light ablaze.

"Let's go," Artemisa instructed, as they watched the bills burn.

"Is that enough petrol?" Lily asked as they walked.

"Yeah, it'll burn," Artemisa said, careful to avert Lily's eyes away from where the bodies lay.

Artemisa's eyes were heavy as she drove. When they arrived back at the hotel, Artemisa remained in the driver's seat, eyes closed, head resting on the steering wheel.

Lily stayed next to her, gently rubbing her back. "You're stressed, let's get you to bed."

When they got into their hotel room, Artemisa threw her clothes on the floor and curled up under the duvet and was asleep as soon as she felt Lily's arms around her, wrapping her up tightly.

Artemisa tossed and turned, and when she woke up it was to find Lily awake, watching Artemisa struggle to remain asleep.

Artemisa muttered a feeble apology before slumping her head back down on the pillows.

"What is troubling you?" Lily asked, poking Artemisa's arm.

"I think I'm just impatient, I want this shit over with."

"You've already accomplished so much over a short space of time. Magaldi needs to put things in motion to make killing him a realistic possibility. Remember your plan, remember the strategy and remember that nothing is going to go wrong."

Artemisa groaned before eventually saying. "You're right. Personal growth is fucking exhausting."

"What do you mean?"

"Life was similar when I believed the propaganda I was fed by the government; when I thought I was doing the right thing. Life was easier when I was with Magaldi, I didn't need to think, I didn't need to plan. I just did as I was told."

"That is the years of control and manipulation talking," Lily pointed out, sitting up a little to look at Artemisa.

Artemisa sighed but did not say anything.

"You know that, right? Regardless of how you feel about killing, not killing, or the people you have killed, you've been manipulated since birth to kill for the reasons given to you. These kills are the first you've done off your own back, for your own reasons, of your own free will."

Artemisa opened her eyes and looked at Lily. It took her a while to find the words she wanted to say. In the end, Artemisa gave up the idea of trying to speak and instead just took Lily's hand and kissed it.

"You don't even need to find something to say," Lily said, smiling, lying back down on her pillows. "I am always right."

Artemisa smiled before eventually drifting back off to sleep. When she awoke it was early, and she was ready for her morning workouts. She was by no means refreshed, but at least today she could get back to work and get that one step closer to her freedom.

When she returned to her hotel room to see Lily just waking up, they showered and left the hotel for brunch. Artemisa led them to a bar and grill and they seated themselves at a window seat.

As they sat down, Artemisa unfurled copies of the morning papers to see if any of her activities had made the news, but she was doubtful. Magaldi would not want to appear vulnerable, so he ordered the police and his own men investigating what was happening to keep quiet. Artemisa knew better than to go after corrupt cops; no, they would need to get their come-uppance a different way.

"Why this bar and grill? Is it work-related at the same time?" Lily whispered, as Artemisa's eyes scanned.

Artemisa nodded as the waiter brought over their drinks, then she eventually said, "We start with the big guns now, we cannot do that on an empty stomach."

"So why here specifically?"

Artemisa nodded across the street where there was an Italian restaurant.

"I see, a Magaldi favourite?"

"One of his, but this one is so much more than just a fine dining Italian restaurant. Keep your eye out for a big, bald bastard in a sharp suit," Artemisa said, her cup of tea inches from her mouth.

They took their time eating brunch and drinking their tea, waiting for the restaurant to open. They saw chefs and servers arrive but no big, bald bastard in a sharp suit.

Eventually, Lily nudged Artemisa and pointed to the dictionary definition of a big, bald bastard in a sharp suit, who entered the restaurant from the main entrance.

"That is him," Artemisa said, getting up from the table. "Be back soon."

"Be safe," Lily whispered, before kissing Artemisa gently on the cheek.

Artemisa crossed the street and walked round the back of the building, surveying her possible entry options. The kitchen door was shut tight, and had a closed window, which Artemisa began peering through.

She only knew the big, bald bastard in the sharp suit as Tony, or 'The Barber'. He was neither a barber nor proficient with a blade. She never knew the origins of the name, only that it was fucking stupid. He stood in the kitchen talking to the head chef.

This head chef was very different to most head chefs in a New York restaurant, as he was the only head chef that Artemisa had seen cut up a human body and feed it to truffle pigs. The last time she had seen the chef or Tony was mere moments before she left the employment of Magaldi.

Artemisa couldn't fit through the window even if it was open, and the door was closed, so the only way into the kitchen that Artemisa could see was to knock on the door.

It was a stupid idea, it was a reckless idea, it gave away all tactical advantage, but it was the only idea Artemisa had. So Artemisa slid her rings from her fingers and put them in her jacket pocket, before removing the jacket and slinging it over a nearby post.

She walked up to the door and rapped her knuckles against it and stepped back, just out of sight.

The head chef, Jeb, opened the door, and peered around the corner. Artemisa yanked his arm towards her and as he stumbled, he fell into her swinging fist. He crumpled to the ground and Artemisa dragged him behind the bins.

"Jeb, what the fuck are you doing out there?" Tony the Barber called from inside the kitchen.

Artemisa stepped in the doorway and said, "He is taking out the trash."

"You," he said simply, as Artemisa closed the door.

"Me."

"Do you really want to do this, little girl?" he leered, cracking his knuckles, as if that gave him any advantage. "I've waited for this, I begged Mr Magaldi to let me kill you."

"You couldn't kill me in my sleep." Artemisa laughed, a dangerous, threatening laugh.

Tony the Barber had the height advantage, weight advantage, size advantage, and Artemisa had lost the element of surprise; the suit and gloves he was wearing meant Artemisa had very little exposed skin to aim at.

Artemisa darted forward, launching two quick punches. Tony blocked one and the other clipped his elbow.

He swung two vicious punches into her ribs, in quick succession. The first knocked the wind out of her and the second dropped her to her knees.

Artemisa had no time to think about the pain. She launched an uppercut, which connected with his groin, and another punch to his knee as his hands shot at her throat.

This brought them back to a level playing field as he dropped to his knees. Artemisa threw three quick punches and Tony the Barber slumped backward. Artemisa emptied his pockets before getting to her feet, looking at the body on the kitchen floor with distaste etched on her face.

She swayed, attempting to regain her balance before wheezing out of the kitchen door, her ribs in agony, and short of breath. She collected her jacket and walked down the street. She saw Lily leave the bar and grill, and they walked for a few minutes before hailing a taxi to take them to Central Park.

"How are your ribs?" Lily asked, lifting Artemisa's t-shirt to look at her ribs.

"Sensitive, cracked." Artemisa winced.

"Let me see," Lily insisted.

"It's fine," Artemisa assured her, despite feeling bruises forming.

"Let's sit and people watch, rest for a bit," Lily suggested.

Artemisa agreed, so they got cups of tea and coffee and sat, Artemisa slouching to take the weight off her ribs.

"Is there more business to take care of?" Lily asked, in a low voice.

"Maybe," Artemisa said, taking Tony's phone out of her jacket pocket. "If we do, it won't be until after sunset."

"So we have until sunset-"

"To do whatever you want," Artemisa said, finishing Lily's

sentence.

After a while, Lily led Artemisa on a path of her own choosing and they walked hand in hand, enjoying the natural beauty.

Chapter Eighteen:

As the sun began to fade, Lily asked Artemisa, "What is the plan?"

"We are going to LaGuardia Airport," Artemisa said, smiling.

"All my stuff is at the hotel!" Lily exclaimed.

"We aren't flying, don't worry," Artemisa soothed.

"Then why are we heading there?"

"Fabiana Magaldi will be flying in from Chicago."

"Why do we know she is flying in now as opposed to already being here?"

"I've checked Tony's phone and she isn't here yet," Artemisa explained as they walked. "But also, Fabiana is a paranoid motherfucker. She barely leaves her house during daylight, let alone her city. So, if she is to fly as the text messages suggest, then she'll fly when the sun is setting and land during darkness."

"Are you sure you're in a fit state to do this?" Lily queried, looking at Artemisa's free hand, which was placed gingerly on her ribs.

"I'll be fine, don't worry," Artemisa reassured her. This of course was redundant as Lily was worried, Artemisa could tell.

"The murder of Tony the Barber will trigger emergency meetings. Magaldi will be paranoid, he'll want his sister here, this makes everything easier," Artemisa explained to Lily after a prolonged silence.

The taxi to the airport reminded Artemisa why she hated New York traffic so much. As they sat in traffic and the sky darkened outside, Artemisa showed Lily a photo of Fabiana Magaldi that Tony the Barber had saved.

"She is pretty," Lily said, "but looks like she is a bitch."

"You've described her to a tee," Artemisa chuckled.

Once they arrived at the airport, they stood waiting for her to arrive.

"Is the plan to kill her here or follow her?" Lily whispered, as they awaited arrivals.

"It's a good question," Artemisa said, looking at the security cameras all around the airport.

"There is a Chicago plane due to land in 15 minutes," Lily said, consulting the board.

"She should be on this one," Artemisa reasoned, "she won't be alone, though."

"Did you get much information from the phone?"

"Some, not a lot. We don't need too much for this."

They began watching people file through from the bag

collection and security, as Lily grabbed Artemisa's arm and said in an excited hush, "I have a plan. When we see her, go into the bathroom. I'll then spill something on her so she'll go into the bathroom to wipe herself down; you can grab her, away from the cameras and away from the people she is with."

Artemisa didn't like the plan, the worst part about it was that it was a really good plan. Fabiana loved looking the part and couldn't do that with a stain. However, she didn't want Lily to get herself in danger.

"You know it is a good plan," Lily muttered.

Artemisa bit her lip but didn't say anything, watching the people walk through to the arrivals area.

Lily saw her before Artemisa did and she said, "Go to the bathroom. Now."

Before Artemisa could say or do anything, Lily had darted towards the shop in the arrivals area.

Artemisa cursed under her breath as she headed to the bathroom. She checked the stalls, which were empty, and she stood at the furthest sink, slowly and methodically running her hands under the hot water, waiting, her heart beating against her bruised rib cage.

The wait was agonising, as Artemisa kept her head down looking at the running water.

The door slammed open and swung back as Artemisa

heard the expensive shoes click and clack on the tiled floor as Fabiana walked in, cursing, "Silly bitch should have watched where she was going."

Artemisa looked at the woman via the mirrors above the sink. She had the visual confirmation she needed, so it was time to move before anyone else used the bathroom.

Artemisa dried her hands and walked behind Fabiana as if she were making her way to the door.

Fabiana looked into the mirror and her eyes widened as she saw Artemisa, but she was not quick enough to react. Artemisa cupped a hand over her mouth, grabbed her and dragged her into a stall.

Fabiana threw her weight back, slamming Artemisa's ribs into the back of the toilet. Artemisa let out a gasp of pain, but the futile fight that Fabiana was putting up was in vain, as she, like so many before, succumbed to Artemisa's touch. Artemisa didn't bother to look at the now deceased Fabiana. Instead, she locked the door to the stall as Fabiana's body slumped on the toilet. Artemisa borrowed everything she needed from Fabiana's purse before she placed her feet between Fabiana's legs on the toilet lid and vaulted into the next cubicle. Once free from the cubicle, she washed her hands and left the bathroom.

Artemisa and Lily left the airport quickly, got in a taxi and headed back to the hotel.

Artemisa and Lily sat in their usual corner of the hotel bar, Lily with a cocktail and Artemisa with a pint of cider, her ribs still in agony. They were two drinks in before either of them began discussing business, when Lily eventually said, "So who else do we have to deal with?"

"Nicoletta and Magaldi himself," Artemisa explained, swirling her glass around her fingers.

"Who is this Nicoletta?"

"Magaldi's second in command, his lawyer. She oversees the work of Tony the Barber, and keeps Fabiana in Chicago, and makes sure people do as they're fucking told."

"She seems important, why have we not dealt with her before?"

"Because she is the one I am hoping Magaldi believes is behind this," Artemisa said, draining her glass. "I am hoping in the way I've gone about things he believes it is a coup and not revenge."

"Oooooh, that's smart," Lily said, smiling.

"Not sure how well it will work, so we are going to focus on Magaldi for now, which isn't a good thing."

"Why?"

"I am fucking good at my job," Artemisa laughed, getting up and heading to the bar to order them more drinks.

When Artemisa returned from the bar, Lily said, "Do we have a plan?"

"Not really, I'll need to consult everything I wrote at the time. We will do that tomorrow."

With business taken care of for the evening, they ordered drinks before heading up to their room and to bed.

Artemisa awoke early in the night. She moved closer to Lily and fell quickly back to sleep, cursing when her alarm woke up for her morning workout.

The workout was brutal and Artemisa was relieved when she stepped into the scorching hot shower. Once she was showered, she slumped into a chair and began reading from the notebook she had written in, what felt like a lifetime ago.

Artemisa had planned for every eventuality; lockdown procedures, escape routes, assassination attempts. She had planned and strategised for everything in order to keep Magaldi alive. Here Artemisa was faced with a paradoxical conundrum - would she, with no plan, be able to beat her best-laid plans? Could the Artemisa of the present beat the Artemisa of over a year and a half ago?

Lily stirred, and Artemisa closed the book and the phones she had 'borrowed' from Fabiana and Tony, but Lily simply rolled over and went back to sleep, so Artemisa continued to scheme.

She had built a safe room. She had installed bullet-resistant glass, installed the security cameras; convinced Magaldi to buy the building his penthouse was on the top floor of, so extra security could be brought in at a moment's notice. Part of Artemisa wished she had done a worse job.

Chapter Nineteen:

As Artemisa pored over her notes, she cursed her brilliance so loudly it caused Lily to stir again. Artemisa was staring at the top right-hand corner of the notebook where she had written five words in a hasty scribble: *Omega clearance, just in case.* With these five words, Artemisa began to formulate a plan with lightning speed.

"What are you smiling at?" Lily yawned.

"How cute you look asleep," Artemisa responded, quickly looking up.

Lily stuck up a middle finger as she put her head back down on the pillows. "What is the plan?"

"Given the fact you're yawning, the plan is for you to go back to sleep?"

"I am up, I am awake," Lily yawned.

"If that is the case, then we have some clothes shopping to do," Artemisa said, a smirk on her face, as she watched Lily's eyes shoot open as she leapt from the bed, all tiredness forgotten.

"I'll get showered and ready."

Artemisa rolled her eyes as Lily raced to the bathroom, before she grabbed a fresh sheet of paper and began shuffling all the relevant information she had taken from the notes and everything she stored securely in her safety deposit box.

"So what kind of shopping are we going for?" Lily asked, as they left the hotel.

"I need a suit and you either need a suit or dress, your snazzy dungarees won't cut it on this occasion."

"Dress," Lily corrected.

"I need a suit and you need a dress," Artemisa smirked.

Artemisa bought the first suit she tried on. It was a sharp, tight-fitting suit with matching sunglasses, and Artemisa couldn't help but smile as she looked at herself in the mirror. She liked wearing suits and she looked damn good doing it.

Lily spent a lot longer looking at dresses, skirts and shirts, trying on different outfits.

"You're going to have to pick one soon, my heart rate can't get any higher, you're making me spike at dangerous levels," Artemisa smirked, as Lily came out of the fitting room in her 13th outfit.

"Fuck off."

"Honestly, look!" Artemisa said, showing Lily the watch.

"I think I've chosen," Lily said, ignoring Artemisa.

"You look amazing in everything you've tried," Artemisa said genuinely.

Once they were changed, Artemisa paid for their outfits and they began to drive out of the city; Artemisa found it difficult to keep her eyes on the road and not on Lily.

"So why do we need the outfits?"

"Suits were how Magaldi expected me to dress when I worked for him."

"Suave, sexy and intimidating?"

"Pretty much, it is about image, what you represent."

"And what part am I here to play?"

"You are going to act the part of Magaldi's next secretary."

"Okay, what are we going to do?"

"We're going to update some security information," Artemisa said, not divulging any more as she hadn't formulated much more of the plan.

The drive took two hours and they eventually pulled into a car park in the centre of an industrial park.

They walked towards the entrance, Artemisa buttoning up her suit jacket. She held the door open for Lily, and they walked into a reception.

"Hi, how can we help you today?" a smiling receptionist greeted.

Artemisa unbuttoned her jacket slowly before she spoke, attempting to be as intimidating as possible. "We are here to see Gareth Elis."

"Is he expecting you?" she asked, her smile fading.

"Tell him, Mr Magaldi's representatives are here."

"Understood," she said, her smile faded completely.

"Representatives of Mr Magaldi? We weren't expecting you," Mr Elis said 10 minutes later.

"Mr Magaldi keeps his cards close to his chest, as is the nature of one's personal security," Artemisa said, "I trust you remember me?"

"This way," he said nervously.

Artemisa and Lily followed Mr Elis towards his office. Lily sat, Artemisa stood behind Lily, her fingers gripped on the back of Lily's chair. Mr Elis closed his office door and took a seat.

After consulting his notes, he said, "What can I assist you with, Artemisa?"

Artemisa and Lily noticed beads of sweat beginning to trickle down the bald man's head.

"Mr Magaldi would like to update the details for his security."

"Of course, is it the iris scanner, or fingerprints, or the

keys he is looking to update?" he asked, his voice shaking.

"My iris imprint is to remain in place, the fingerprints are to be removed and the keys are to be carried by his new assistant, Florence," Artemisa said, taking a step closer and indicating Lily.

"I understand your omega level access is to remain in place as well?"

"Correct," Artemisa said, "as are the non-disclosure agreements, unless, of course, I die."

"I will need your scan in order to do this," he said, whimpering slightly.

Artemisa took off her sunglasses and Mr Elis flinched as he saw the glare Artemisa was giving him.

They removed the fingerprints from the system, updated Artemisa's iris scanner, and signed the relevant paperwork for the keys to be handed over to Lily.

When they had taken care of everything, they bid the quivering man good day and left.

When they were back in the car and driving away, Lily let out a laugh and said, "Holy fuck, you were so intense."

"Nah, that wasn't intense, he is just a very frightened man."

"So what have we just done?"

"Made it so that if Magaldi enters his panic room, only I can open it."

"Could you not enter it before?"

"Yes, but I wouldn't have been the only one, they weren't my fingerprints set up."

"Why not?"

"I don't have any fingerprints," Artemisa said, stretching her fingers on the steering wheel.

"Excuse me?" Lily said, reaching for one of Artemisa's hands.

Artemisa allowed her to examine her fingers with a bemused look on her face. "They got burned off when I was a child."

"By accident?"

"No of course not, they did it on purpose, so I don't leave fingerprints anywhere."

"That is sick," Lily said, repulsed.

"Smart, and makes life a lot easier," Artemisa reasoned as they drove.

They listened to music for much of the journey. Artemisa found the silence soothing and it meant she could avoid discussing the rest of the plan, because she didn't have a plan and that was concerning her.

Eventually, Lily asked the question, "So what is next?"

"I don't know," Artemisa answered honestly.

"How do we get to Magaldi?"

"It might be impossible," Artemisa admitted.

"Why? Tell me why it might be impossible."

"Magaldi will be locked in his penthouse. He will have extra security, he will have snipers on the rooftops opposite, overlooking the penthouse, ensuring that if anything happens, they're there to guarantee his safety. Not to mention the security that will be in the apartment, I would have no element of surprise, I would be dead before I even got to him."

Lily pondered this, as Artemisa returned her attention to navigating the New York traffic.

"What are the ways to get into the penthouse?"

"Door or private elevator."

"The elevator to the penthouse-"

"Requires a key that I don't have," Artemisa said, finishing Lily's sentence for her.

They brainstormed ideas in the hotel bar for most of the evening, Lily getting more enthusiastic with each idea, Artemisa getting more disgruntled with each idea.

"What about, if you evacuated the building, and then we're in the apartment waiting for him?"

Artemisa looked up from her glass, thinking about this idea. "Would gain the element of surprise, doesn't account for the snipers."

"They'd be trained on the evacuation, so you could slip inside."

"I'll think about it tomorrow," Artemisa sighed, not wanting to discuss it any longer

"You need to stop avoiding this," Lily advised sternly.

"I'm not avoiding anything."

"Oh, you so are," Lily said, not believing what Artemisa was saying.

They went up to bed shortly after, and although Artemisa didn't want to discuss it, she could not get to sleep plagued with thoughts and schemes and a crippling anxiety. This, coupled with the pain in her ribs, meant by the time Artemisa's alarm went off the next morning, she was more exhausted than when she first went to sleep.

Her morning workout was also hampered by her bad ribs, and she eventually gave it up as a bad job and returned to the hotel room. Lily was still asleep, and Artemisa resigned herself to poring over the documents that she could memorise at this point; she didn't know what more she could do.

She went down to get breakfast when Lily began to stir. Artemisa walked through New York looking for something to take her fancy. In the end she decided on bagels, so she joined a queue of people.

As Artemisa got closer to the counter, she could hear the staff complaining about a delivery order that was coming through. "I fucking hate having to deliver to THAT office, the security are always throbbers, just let me go up and deliver to the boardroom, that way at least I get a tip. I'd prefer to deliver to the law firm only."

"I know, so many businesses are okay with it, it's just them who are throbbers, at least the sleazebag lawyers tip well."

Artemisa snorted at them being called throbbers as she got to the front, and when she saw the uniform the staff were wearing, the cogs started turning and Artemisa began to formulate a plan.

Lily was awake and in the shower when Artemisa returned with their breakfast, so Artemisa began to think about how to evacuate the whole building before making her move into Magaldi's apartment.

"Breakfast?" Lily asked, exiting the bathroom.

"Eat up," Artemisa said, taking a bagel for herself and offering one to Lily.

"You look like you've had an idea?" Lily said, over the

noise of the hairdryer.

Artemisa nodded but waited for Lily's hair to be dry before answering, "It is half of a plan."

Once they had eaten their fill of bagels, they left the hotel and Artemisa began scheming.

"What are we looking for?" Lily asked.

"There," Artemisa said, pointing to a print and embroidery shop. "I knew I saw one the other day."

"What are we doing here?"

"Getting me my ticket into the building, no questions asked."

Artemisa purchased a t-shirt and baseball cap embroidered with a simple logo she scribbled down and the words 'Allie's doughnuts, sprinkle your way to happiness', a rip off of the logo and slogan of a doughnut shop she passed the other day.

"So the plan is to walk into the building through the front door because of the logo on your t-shirt and cap?" Lily asked.

"Exactly, delivery for one of the rooms. It's simple, gets me in the building, no questions asked. Only thing to figure out now is getting everybody else out of the building."

"Rather than attempting to figure out how to set a fire, why not figure out how to sabotage the fire alarm system, that way it's less suspicious than setting fire to something?"

"Yeah, it is… the only issue is that I cannot remember where the alarm setting is."

"Surely all you would need would be to damage a cable?"

"Potentially, I am probably just going to wing it."

"Okay, so that is getting you in and getting everyone else out, but what about when you're in the flat. There will still be snipers, won't there?"

"Let's hope I am better at not getting shot than I think I am." Artemisa laughed.

"You're joking, right?" Lily asked, laughing, "Artemisa, you're joking right?"

"Of course I am joking," Artemisa replied.

"So what is the plan?"

"Avoid the bullets. Kill the man. Don't get shot," she said confidently.

"Yeah, babe. I think we need a better plan than 'avoid bullets and don't get shot'. Like a real plan."

"I don't have a real plan, so this is what we are doing."

"What am I to do?"

"You are going to speak to a news reporter, anonymously drop off a dossier, memory stick, every piece of evidence that we have. Then go to another hotel, closer to JFK airport. Once this is over then we can go somewhere and be free together."

"I think you're oversimplifying everything. What is this dossier?"

"Maybe, maybe not, but there is only so much I can do from a hotel room. The time to act is now, we are going to create the dossier now. Bringing down the Magaldi crime empire means bringing down half of New York as well."

Chapter Twenty:

Artemisa spent much of the day compiling everything she had on the Magaldi crime empire; the shell corporations, the money trials, the corruption and the power grab that Artemisa had facilitated. She obviously kept her name out of everything but along with the memory stick from the cinema, she had enough to cause some lasting damage.

As it darkened, Artemisa changed into her t-shirt and baseball cap, tucked her knife into the slot in her boot, put on a backpack and kissed Lily, handing her the documents.

"Lily, I'll be fine. I'll be back with you soon, my love."

Lily nodded as Artemisa handed her the keys to their rental car as she left the room, heading towards Magaldi's apartment.

Artemisa stopped off and bought doughnuts to make the part authentic. Artemisa began to shake as she readjusted the glasses she was wearing; she was five minutes away from everything.

As Artemisa walked, her legs began to feel heavy. She was realising what she was about to do, everything since she wanted to leave had led to this point, whether she was aware of it or not, it all came down to this decision. Artemisa, the instrument of death, was about to do something for her.

Artemisa was about to end a dynasty that, when she had helped to put it in place, she had expected to stay for generations. Whatever she built, she could destroy. Artemisa allowed herself a wry smile.

She entered the building and gave the concierge a wide smile. "I'm here to sprinkle the way to happiness for someone," she recited, pointing at her hat with the logo.

"Do you have to say that every time you do a delivery?"

"Unfortunately," Artemisa said, rolling her eyes, "Do you mind if I take the stairs? Get my steps up."

"Go for it."

"You're a saint," Artemisa said, walking towards the stairs. Once she was out of sight of the people at the entrance and the cameras, she headed down to the underground car park.

She began scanning the walls for any cabling, or indeed a fire alarm that was not in sight of the security camera. She found one and made her way towards it.

Artemisa knew she would have to run at the wall, leap off it to get the height and then jab her knife at the fire alarm cable, hoping to set it off, at which point she would wait until the building was evacuated before making her move.

It took three attempts for Artemisa to set off the fire alarm. She took off her backpack and squatted behind a car, out of sight of the security camera and out of sight of anyone who might come down to the underground parking.

She heard the sound of hundreds of people beginning to make their way down the stairs and out the exits. She waited patiently and as the last footsteps stopped and only the sound of the fire alarm remained, Artemisa took a deep, steadying breath. She placed a hand on her ribs and began to run up the stairs, cursing the fact that she couldn't use the elevator.

When she eventually made her way to Magaldi's penthouse, she was breathing deeply. She twisted her baseball cap round so it sat backwards, and began opening the door with the keys she and Lily had got, and used her iris scan to open the door.

She slipped into the apartment and began to edge round, surveying the room. It was as grandiose as ever. Magaldi had commissioned a portrait of himself in the year since she was last in this room, which hung above the fireplace, but the room felt familiar and Artemisa vowed she would never set foot in the room after tonight.

She knew her best bet was to get Magaldi alone, and to do that she would need to spook him. So she cautiously made her way across to the drinks cabinet and made herself a drink, leaving an ice cube on the silver tray.

Artemisa made her way to the bedroom and sat in the shadows, eating a doughnut as she waited. She sat in the darkness for an hour and forty-five minutes until she finally heard footsteps below her, and the fire engines that had been dispatched returned to the station.

Artemisa felt anxious as she heard people begin to re-enter the building. She didn't know when Magaldi would arrive but with the presence of people outside, it was highly probable that he was here.

Artemisa moved to the shadows when the door opened. Three men entered, followed by Magaldi. Artemisa let out a small gasp. They were finally in the same room; they were face to face at last, or would be soon enough.

"I want them to ensure that this NEVER happens again. A technical issue? I don't pay for technical issues."

"Understood, sir, I'll get the entire building system reviewed tomorrow," Artemisa heard one of them say.

Artemisa saw Magaldi's eyes focus on the ice cube and she readied herself for a fight. What she did not and could not ready herself for was Magaldi saying, "Send the boys home, and the snipers, it has been a long night."

"Are you sure, sir?"

"Yes, go down to the normal level."

"Understood, sir."

Artemisa watched them leave the room and waited, her heart beating against her bruised ribs, and she let out an involuntary shudder and waited.

"Artemisa, you can come out from wherever you are

hiding."

"You knew it was me?" Artemisa asked, exiting the bedroom.

"When I saw the ice cube, yes," he said, indicating the melting cube. "Only you would have been able to access the penthouse, it is a shame. Now Nicoletta lies dead in her car as we believed she was the one behind all of this."

"Seems you got to her before I did."

"Oh, I believe you left her alive for me to kill for that very reason, cover your tracks."

"And yet, when you guessed it was me you sent everyone home, why?"

"Because if I knew it was you, I wouldn't have spent so much on security."

"I would have thought you would have spent more?" Artemisa queried, stepping closer to Magaldi. "You should have learnt by now that I do not give a shit about business."

"We'll see, we'll see but watch your language," Magaldi said, not looking at her, putting a log on the fire and heading towards the drinks cabinet. "You'll allow me a cigar, glass of red and a conversation?"

"Sure," Artemisa said, cautiously, accepting a cigar and a large Knob Creek whiskey on the rocks.

"So, you planned everything? Planned all of this? All the

misfortune recently, it has not been someone attempting to take over my empire, it has been you."

"Killing the father of New York is no easy task," Artemisa admitted. "I am too good at what I do for that to be easy."

"Oh, are you going to kill me?" he asked, an eyebrow raised and a hint of surprise in his voice.

"You think I went through all this effort for a Cuban cigar and a glass of my favourite whiskey?"

"Why kill me? Why go through all of this?"

"Have you forgotten? I asked for one favour, after everything I did to build this empire on your behalf and when my work was done, I wanted out. You refused."

"I couldn't have you working for another family."

"I said I was done, I was retiring. Yet you told the Feds I was alive."

"Yes... I did do that."

"For that, you forfeit your right to live."

"A small mistake. Artemisa, you need to think bigger."

Artemisa let out a harsh, fake laugh before she growled, "Small mistake? A small mistake? You told the C.I.A. I was still alive, you made me enemy number one, hunted day and night."

"So?" he asked, almost sounding bored. "You can instantly kill people?"

"I am tired of killing people, I want a quiet life and you took that from me."

"You are the ultimate instrument of death; you build empires, topple empires, topple governments, topple countries. That is your purpose. You cannot walk away from your destiny."

"My destiny is my own, you should have realised I cannot be controlled or owned, if you would have let me go then I would have left your empire untouched."

"I presumed that you would come back for the same reason you won't kill me. Purpose. For so long you have gone from one mission to another, having your purpose told to you and following orders, one hit list after another. Without a purpose, without a mission, you would go insane."

"So what? You now invite me back into the fold? Back into the Magaldi family?"

"With open arms."

"Finish your wine," Artemisa sighed.

"You kill me, do you really think you walk out of this building alive?"

"Yeah, I think I have a pretty good chance. I'm smarter than you give me credit for. I have always had an insurance policy."

"Oh really?" he sneered.

"Yeah," Artemisa said, showing him her watch. "My heart rate drops to zero and my hired associate, who is sitting outside a house with the number of 741, breaks in and murders the occupant in a robbery."

"You threaten my mother?" he whispered, the sneer and the arrogance was gone, there was only hatred, dangerous hatred in his voice now.

"As I said, insurance policy," Artemisa shrugged. "The past year on the run, I've spent a long time on trains and planes, I got bored and consequently have spent a lot of time reading. Some history and some philosophy here and there. Know what I have learned?"

"Enlighten me?"

"Tyrants, dictators, crime bosses. They are all the architects of their own downfall. You engineered your own death."

"You think of me as a dictator?"

"I think you engineered your own downfall. Who takes over when you are dead?"

"The Magaldi family will always run New York."

"Maybe, maybe not. One thing that is certain, whoever runs New York will not know that I exist and if they know I exist then they will know not to fuck with me."

Magaldi drained the remainder of the wine and picked up the bottle, looking longingly at the label. "Such a good year," he sighed, "it's time you accepted my offer and left, I am tired."

"I admire your optimism in the face of death, Roman, I really do."

Magaldi's face turned from the bottle to look at Artemisa, she could see him enraged by the disrespect.

Artemisa smiled, "Roman Magaldi, you came into the world kicking and screaming, exit it the same way."

"You're a fool, Artemisa, throwing it all away and for what? For you to never leave this building alive?"

"Neither will you," she said, standing up and placing her cigar in the ashtray.

She admired the balls of the old man, to dart at her with a flip knife. She moved out of the way, and couldn't help but smile as she grabbed his arm and prised the knife from his fingers.

She pushed him away and waited to see his next move, inviting him closer. When she saw his next move, she decided to end it early.

"That is just cheating," Artemisa said, as she saw Magaldi draw a revolver from his hip. She dived at him, knocking him off balance. As they fell, Magaldi pulled the trigger and Artemisa let out a roar as she felt the bullet rip into her thigh.

Artemisa desperately began to push the pain to the back

of her mind. She let out deep steadying breaths, as she used her good leg to push herself across the wooden floor towards him.

She wrapped a hand around his throat and punched him repeatedly in the face before he could fire again. He eventually stopped squirming and Artemisa released his neck and began to pull herself up to her feet, using the armchair she was sitting in before.

Artemisa bit her lip until she could taste blood in her mouth. Her ribs did not appreciate the fall to the floor. Blood ran down her leg as Artemisa struggled to Magaldi's bedroom. Now he was dead and there was no danger, the pain in her thigh was becoming excruciating and Artemisa let out a yelp of pain. She began tying Magaldi's neckties around her leg in order to stop the bleeding.

The bullet was not through and through and Artemisa didn't know if that made things better or worse. Her eyes began to water as she tied six neckties around her thigh. She felt her leg going stiff as she borrowed a fine wooden walking cane and Artemisa left.

She took the box of Cubans and the bottle of whiskey and headed towards the panic room. She entered the key and scanned her eye before entering the room.

It hadn't been used, not that Artemisa was surprised. She sealed the door and sat, allowing herself a brief pause to try and not think about the pain in her leg, but it was impossible.

Magaldi's arrogance had led to this, and Artemisa allowed herself a smile as she inserted the keys and selected the basement. She had overseen the installation, refurbishment and building work in the penthouse.

"The panic room also being an escape elevator is stupid, Artemisa, a hidden elevator is a waste of money and stupid, Artemisa. Fuck you, contractor Tim," Artemisa said smugly, recalling a conversation that she had had all that time ago.

When the elevator doors opened to a secret garage, she saw the car she parked there when she finished being Magaldi's personal driver. She opened the doors, turned on the engine and began to drive. The garage doors opened automatically and she drove away, exceedingly glad she was in an automatic and not a manual, as the pain in her leg was brutal. She needed to get her leg stitched up and she needed something for the pain. Above all, she needed to be with Lily again.

Chapter Twenty-One:

She pulled over and began to search the onboard navigation for anywhere that would be sterile. The pain was becoming too much to bear, so Artemisa threw caution to the wind and drove to the nearest sterile place: Dr Ng dental office.

Artemisa half-crawled up the steps, using the stick for as much leverage as possible, and rang the bell. Artemisa was close to throwing up in the five-minute wait it took to be answered by a short, petite woman who said, "Sorry we are currently-" She stopped speaking seeing Artemisa's crimson leg.

"Is the doctor in?" Artemisa asked, as politely as possible.

"You need a hospital."

"I need somewhere sterile and with forceps," Artemisa replied. "I have a lot of fucking cash."

"This way," she said eventually, and Artemisa made her way slowly into the dental lab.

"You should have gone to a vet, they would at least have general anaesthetic."

"No, no pain killers," Artemisa moaned, as she was helped into the dentist's chair.

"Then this is going to fucking hurt. I am going to have to cut you out of your jeans and then I will get the bullet out."

"I love these jeans," Artemisa muttered.

"These ties are expensive. Like really expensive," Dr Ng said, unwrapping them from Artemisa's leg.

"As long as you can get the blood out, then they are yours," Artemisa groaned, as cheerfully as possible.

"Is this your normal reaction to getting shot?" Dr Ng said, not smiling. "Do you know what would happen if I were found to be helping you?"

"You'd receive a good Samaritan award?"

"Take these and then bite on this," Dr Ng said, sliding painkillers over a plastic rubber-looking bar.

Artemisa clenched the rubber bar in her teeth and laid down, ignoring the painkillers.

"You're lucky, it's wedged in the ample thigh muscles," Dr Ng said, beginning to inject her thigh.

Artemisa endured over 15 minutes of agony until Dr Ng said, "You're done, just don't tear the stitching open."

"Thank you, Doctor," Artemisa gasped, reaching into her bag and taking out the cash she had taken from Magaldi's apartment. "Tell me when to stop."

Artemisa began putting fifty-dollar bills onto the clean counter. after a few hundred dollars, "You can stop there, if I never see you again," Dr Ng said, cautiously.

"Deal."

Artemisa leaned heavily on the stick, she bid them farewell and began heading towards her car.

The drive towards the hotel near JFK airport was a slow and painful one, Artemisa not wanting to drive fast or risk being pulled over.

When she eventually arrived, she rang Lily who gave her the door number of 619.

Artemisa walked through the empty lobby, very cautious at how odd she must look. She entered the elevator and was soon outside of room 619.

"Lily it's me. Open up," she moaned wearily.

Lily flung the door open and with it, all the colour drained from her beautiful face. She became whiter than snow as she took in Artemisa's odd appearance.

"Oh my God," she whispered. "Oh my God. Oh my God."

"Lily, it's okay," Artemisa whispered, taking Lily's hand as she limped into the hotel room.

Lily looked at the dried blood, bandages, missing jeans leg and walking stick before asking, "What happened?"

"It was a small bullet wound," Artemisa said.

"What do you mean?" she squealed.

"Relax, I've taken care of it, got it stitched up. Nothing to worry about."

Artemisa was forced to sit as Lily began to fret over her,

taking her temperature and checking Artemisa's leg.

"Lily," Artemisa said softly.

"Oh my God, what if it gets infected?" Lily enquired, not hearing Artemisa.

"Lily," Artemisa repeated, a little louder.

"Do we need to dig a bullet out?" Lily said, her voice getting higher.

Artemisa groaned and used the stick to hoist herself up onto her feet. She kept her injured leg elevated and leant forward and gave Lily a gentle kiss.

"Lily, it is okay. It is stitched up. I need a bath and some rest, and you need to not worry. I promised you I would be okay, and I am okay."

"Right, bath," Lily said, now colour was returning to her face, she was blushing.

Artemisa sank gratefully into the bath once it was full, and let out a groan; the steam rose into Lily's face.

Artemisa closed her eyes as she listened to Lily and began to slow her breathing to take away the pain in her leg.

"You better not be asleep; we need to get your leg clean and then you can sleep," Lily said.

"I am awake, it's just soothing listening to the sound of your voice."

"You need to put your leg under the water," Lily said,

gently pressing Artemisa's thigh under the water. Artemisa let out a hiss.

"How does it feel?" Lily asked, as she began to splash and rub water over the dried blood, avoiding the stitches.

"Agony."

"It's over, you've done it. You can rest now, really rest," Lily said soothingly.

"Did you give everything to the newsreader?"

"Yes, she accepted everything. It really is over."

Artemisa began to understand and fully comprehend what Lily had just said, the pain from getting shot driving the realisation out of her mind. It was over, Artemisa was free.

Lily let Artemisa wrap her wet arms around her in a hug as the realisation washed over her, and she allowed herself a moment of weakness as she broke down in Lily's arms.

Eventually Lily aided Artemisa from the bath to their bed and as Artemisa slumped down onto the pillow, she was asleep within minutes.

It was two o'clock in the afternoon when Artemisa awoke, Lily was not next to her or anywhere. As Artemisa began to panic, she saw a note from Lily which read, *'Buying you a new pair of jeans and getting pain killers. Be back soon with lunch x'.*

Artemisa's leg was stiff, and moving around was exhausting and not to mention painful. Artemisa began to think about what direction her life could possibly take now she was truly free. Lily, if she wanted to, was now free to pursue a career in her chosen field without her father's interference, but for her, Artemisa didn't know, she had never thought this far ahead. In the back of her head there was a twinge of panic as Magaldi's words came back to her about her needing a mission and a focus.

Whilst Lily was out Artemisa reminded herself of the only thing she had left to do. Cross off the name of the Magaldi crime family on her kill list

~~C.I.A. Agent Humpfrey Spencer~~

~~MI5 Agent Anthony Houghton~~

~~Polunin Yurievich~~

~~Magaldi Crime Family~~

With the last name crossed out Artemisa let out a triumphant cry before flopping back down onto her pillows, taking deep steadying breaths. She was missing Lily being next to her and pined for her return.

Artemisa let out a grateful sigh of relief when Lily returned shortly after with food, pain killers, more first aid equipment and a pair of loose-fitting jeans and tracksuit bottoms.

"You're the best," Artemisa said, as Lily helped her into the tracksuit bottoms, and she began tucking into the burger.

"You were out like a light, I tried to wake you, but you weren't having any of it," Lily smirked.

"Sorry," Artemisa yawned.

"Don't be sorry, it has been a long few months, it's taken a toll on you."

Artemisa nodded in agreement as they ate the food Lily had bought them.

"What is the plan? Want to go somewhere else in America or back home? The world is ours."

"Are you going to be able to travel on your leg?" Lily asked.

"Not sure, but I also want to leave New York. My leg is painful and really stiff."

"Well, why don't we go up to Toronto? Stop off in Niagara Falls on the way? We did say we wanted to be tourists, enjoy a normal life! And now, we can enjoy our life together."

"That sounds like a good idea," Artemisa agreed, sitting down and stretching her leg out.

"We can rest here till tomorrow at least, leave early in the morning?"

Artemisa would have wanted to leave then and there but after looking at a map, she knew they would need to leave her leg longer to heal.

They went to the hotel bar later that evening for a few drinks and food, and they began to plan the road trip. Artemisa regretted not being able to fight through the pain enough to go to an actual doctor, who could have at least prescribed something to help.

Chapter Twenty-Two:

The next morning, they fuelled their rental, bought everything they would need for the journey and began the drive from New York to Niagara.

Artemisa and Lily took turns driving, Artemisa's leg cramping as she did her best to not tear the stitches by moving or bending her leg. Eventually, in the mid-afternoon they arrived at the border between America and Canada.

The border crossing was slow, but they eventually arrived and made their way towards a swanky-looking hotel. They checked into the hotel and went up to their room.

"Holy shit!" Lily gasped, as she looked out of the window at the view.

"I couldn't get you a view that overlooked the car park, could I?" Artemisa said, beaming as she followed Lily into the room. She stood next to her at the window.

"You're the best," Lily said, kissing her cheek.

Artemisa lay on the bed, admiring the view of Lily and the beautiful natural landscape, and wondered if she ever would have suspected her life would turn out this way; a bullet wound in her thigh aside, Artemisa was feeling pretty happy.

They went out for food that evening, and Artemisa sat with her back against the wall, surveying everything. It was hard to shrug off the feeling that something was going to go wrong.

Lily, however, knew how to calm Artemisa down; she took her hand and reassured her that she had nothing to be concerned about. As their desserts arrived, Artemisa looked across the table at Lily and the realisation sunk in about what this holiday meant. It meant she was free; Japan, Russia, U.K., U.S.A., they were all business trips, whereas this, they had nothing to do but enjoy each other's company. The world was their oyster, and she was free. Free from the manipulative shackles of the U.S. government, from the Magaldi crime family. And everyone who could pose a threat to her was dead.

Artemisa's mind spiralled into the fact that this could literally be her life till she was old and grey. The world was a big place, and it was theirs to explore.

"What are you thinking about?" Lily asked, which brought Artemisa from flying around the world back to their table in Niagara Falls.

Artemisa smiled and told her every thought that had been through her head since they arrived on this side of the Canadian-U.S. border.

"You're a dork," Lily said, as Artemisa paid the bill. "Part of the holiday is not over-thinking, not thinking far ahead, enjoying the here and now."

"Well, we will have to take more holidays for you to teach me these things," Artemisa said, rolling her eyes.

"Fine, maybe we will," Lily replied in a sing-song voice.

When they returned to the hotel, Lily went to the bar to get them some drinks, and Artemisa headed to the reception and booked the boat tour around Niagara Falls, and some other touristy things for them to do over the next few days.

"Ooh how exciting, are you planning on proposing?" the receptionist asked.

"Am I what now?!" Artemisa said, her hand slipping on her walking cane.

"A lot of people who book the boat tour then propose with the waterfall behind them, it's very romantic."

"Thanks," Artemisa said, now walking to the bar wondering if she should propose to Lily, after all they've been through it was extremely unlikely they'd break up.

"What were you booking for us?" Lily asked, as she slid a drink over to Artemisa and moved a chair so Artemisa could put her leg up and rest it.

Artemisa explained everything she booked in at reception, leaving out the thoughts of the receptionist that Artemisa was going to propose.

Lily was excited at the idea, and they spent most of the night discussing plans for the coming days.

When they went to bed that night, Lily fell asleep quickly but Artemisa couldn't sleep, she kept thinking about how far she had come. From her time under the *employment* of the U.S. government, her time working for Magaldi, even from the time she landed exhausted in Japan till now. She was proud of herself and thought that may be the best way to leave her old life behind her for good was with a statement of her defiance, and propose to Lily.

Artemisa got up and, leaving Lily a note saying that she was going to 'stretch her leg', she walked into town, looking for a jewellery store.

Artemisa walked, leaning on her stick and watched the world go by until she found what she was looking for: a fine jewellery shop with necklaces, earrings and rings in the window. Artemisa rang the bell and waited for anyone to come to the door.

"What can I help you with?" a spindly man said.

"I'm looking for an engagement ring," Artemisa explained, the words sounding strange in her mouth.

"Jennifer?" he called over his shoulder.

A woman, slightly older than Artemisa came out from the back and approached Artemisa.

"My apologies about him, I'm still training him to be more accepting of other marriages. What can I help you with today?"

"I'm looking for an engagement ring," Artemisa repeated, glaring daggers at the back of the old man's head who was leaving the front of the shop.

"Excellent, do you know their ring size?"

"About a size smaller than these," Artemisa said, sliding her favourite ring off her finger and showing the woman.

"That is absolutely fine, let's have a look at rings shall we, what is your budget?"

Artemisa shrugged, "Whatever a nice ring costs, that is my budget."

Artemisa looked at every ring intently, not only doing the breath test to ensure the diamonds were real but about the metal they were made from until finally she saw the one. She didn't know what made it the one, but something about it reminded her of Lily's smile.

"A nice choice, it is very beautiful," Jennifer said, taking the ring out of Artemisa's fingers and putting it in a light blue box with a ribbon on it and handed it to Artemisa. "I hope they say yes."

"So do I," Artemisa chuckled, taking cash out of her wallet.

With the ring secure in her pocket, Artemisa headed back to the hotel to find Lily awake, waiting for her so they could go for breakfast.

"How is the leg holding up?" Lily asked her.

"Getting better every day. Are you ready for some food?"

"I'm famished, let's go grab food and then head towards the Falls."

Whilst they were eating four helpings of the hotel's complimentary breakfast, Artemisa and Lily watched the news channels which were all broadcasting the same breaking news story: corruption and bribery within the New York Police Department, F.B.I and C.I.A. Lily and Artemisa were naturally not shocked by this news, having been the whistle-blowers, but it was fascinating to see the fallout happening live; federal officers being dragged out of buildings in handcuffs. Artemisa recognised the woman she had duped on the train platform escaping New York all that time ago sobbing as she was arrested from her family home.

Once they couldn't eat another mouthful, Lily insisted on triple checking the stitches in Artemisa's leg before they left the hotel and headed towards the attraction they were there to see.

Lily stopped and bought a camera so they could take photos. Lily insisted she take photos of Artemisa with the waterfall in the background and they asked a very nice Canadian couple to take a few photos of them.

They bought ponchos to keep their clothes as dry as possible as they boarded the boat to go around the waterfall.

Lily was enjoying taking photos of all of them together, despite the icy coldness of the water spraying on them and the ponchos not doing a great job.

As the boat sailed and the tour guide spoke, Lily and

Artemisa walked to a less crowded area of the boat, near the kind Canadian couple from earlier.

"I've been thinking a lot recently, about you now being free," Lily said, as they looked out across the water.

"So have I," Artemisa said, her hand twitching over the box in her pocket.

"I think you should mark the occasion, in a special way."

"Yeah, that is what I thought," Artemisa said, turning to look at Lily. "I thought about a normal life, a free life and I didn't really know what that was. The only thing I did know was that you were going to be a part of it."

Lily's head tilted curiously as Artemisa, fingers trembling, took the box out of her pocket. She struggled to get down on one knee and said, "Lily, will you spend the rest of your life with me?"

Lily laughed and to Artemisa's amazement she also got down on one knee, pulling a box from her jacket pocket and said, "Only if you'll spend it with me?"

They both looked at the other's rings and grinned, smiles going from ear to ear.

"Yes," they said at the same time, and wrapped each other in a warm hug.

They stood up, Artemisa with Lily's assistance, and noticed the Canadian couple beaming at them and taking photos on a disposable camera, which they gave to Lily.

"I can't believe you proposed at the same time as me, completely stole my thunder," Lily laughed, as Artemisa put the ring on Lily's finger. "You deserve the world, my love."

"If it makes you feel better, I've ripped the stitching in my thigh," Artemisa chuckled.

"You fucking idiot," Lily laughed.

"Your," Artemisa corrected her.

"Huh?"

"I'm your fucking idiot."

"Smile for the photos and then kiss me," Lily said.

They turned, with the waterfall in the background, tears in their eyes and beaming smiles on their faces. The boat sailed towards their new future, a future together, a peaceful life.

ABOUT THE AUTHOR

Daniel is from Manchester, UK. In 2018 he finished his degree in philosophy and politics with a 2:1, his dissertation focusing on 'how recent media attention on sexual harassment has impacted on female empowerment.' In his spare time when not writing he is usually reading or binging tv shows.

Other books by Daniel:

The Adventures of Maddie and Liv (book one)
Joining G.U.A.R.D (book two)
The Final Mission (book 3)

For more information about our books, or to submit your manuscript, please visit our website
www.green-cat.shop